D.L. WINTER

Illustrated by Brian McElligott

Map of Fleurbania by Dmitriy Shvets

September 2, 2022

DLWinterAuthor@gmail.com

Acquisition Editor: Anne Bruce

Editorial Director: Phyllis Jask

Graphic Designer: Brenda Hawkes

Cover Designer: Phil Studdard/Flip Design Studio

Illustrator: Brian McElligott

Map Illustrator: Dmitriy Shvets

Author photos by Shane Boultinghouse

Printed in the United States of America

ISBN-13: 978-10880-45725

FLEURBANIA

Northern Fleurbania
Formerly Brueland

True North

W
E
S

Persicoh

Goldfin Cove

Saint Richarde

Mont Renault

Isle of LaMer

Azlyn Sea

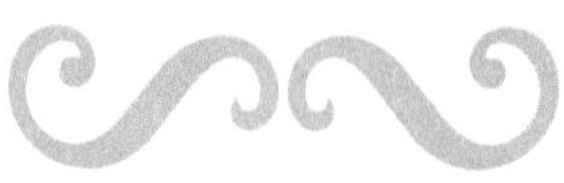

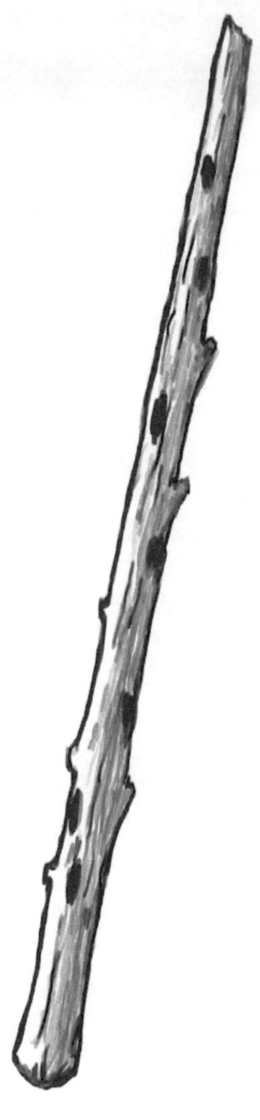

"We all have a little bit of magic inside of us but only those born with a true wizard's gift are capable of gleaning from the wisdom within."

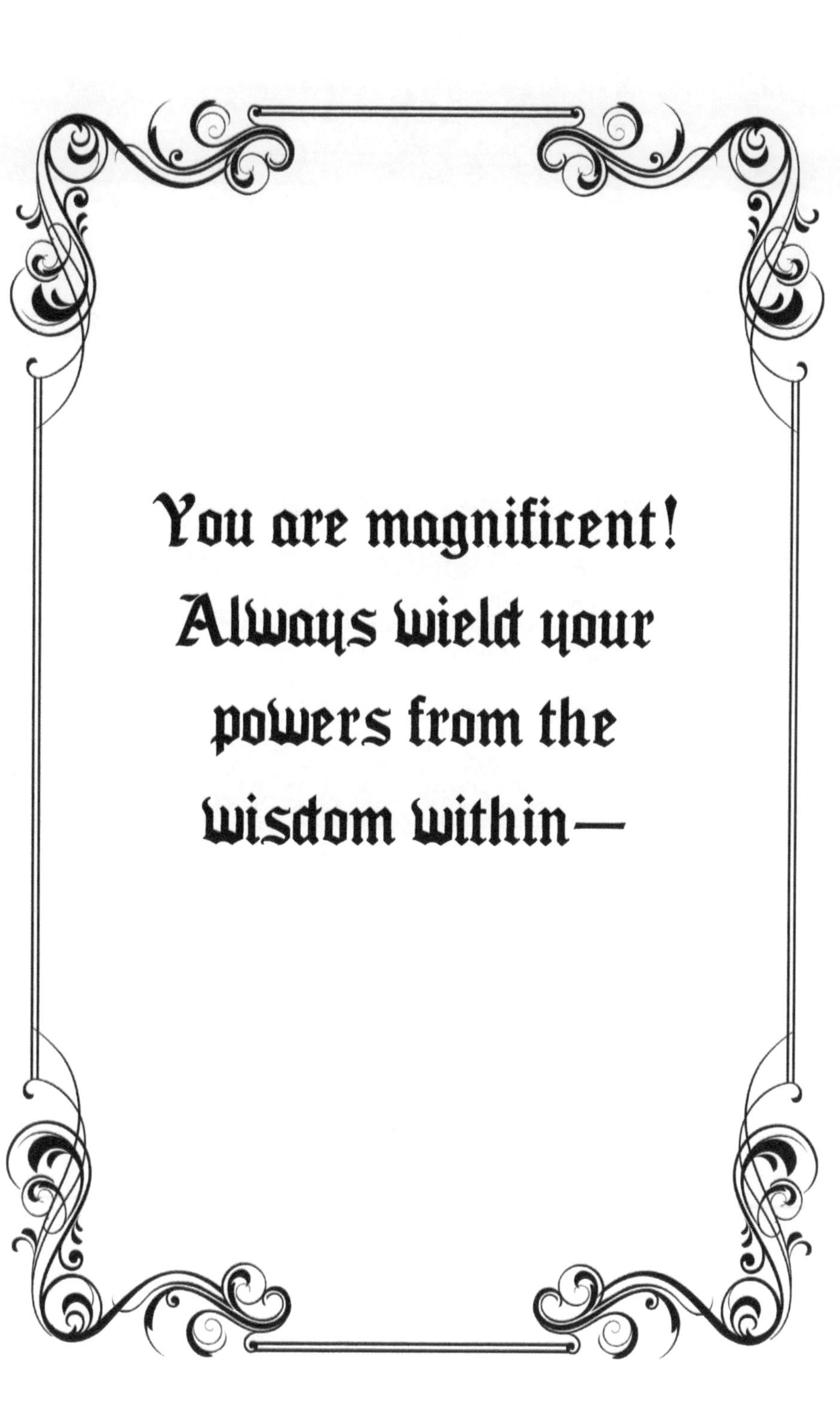

You are magnificent!
Always wield your
powers from the
wisdom within—

For James

CONTENTS

CHAPTER ONE:
Introducing Alistur the Magnificent
1

CHAPTER TWO:
Aristocracy Under the Sea
25

CHAPTER THREE:
Calamities Exposed
47

CHAPTER FOUR:
Fire-Breathing Beasts
57

CHAPTER FIVE:
Conditions of the Agreement
71

CHAPTER SIX:
The Accidental Queen
93

CHAPTER SEVEN:
A Bittersweet Message
111

CHAPTER EIGHT:
Mysterious Jewels
119

CHAPTER NINE:
Complications in the Caverns
129

CHAPTER TEN:
More Complications and Uncertainty
159

CHAPTER ELEVEN:
In the Eye of the Storm
181

CHAPTER TWELVE:
Things Great-Grandfather Used to Say
219

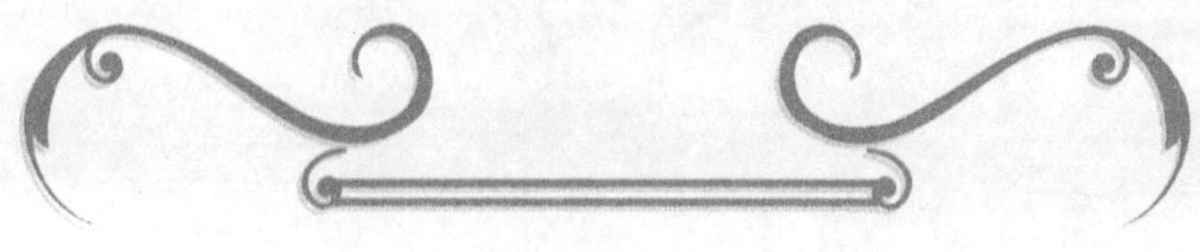

"Imagination is everything. It is the preview of life's coming attractions."

—Albert Einstein

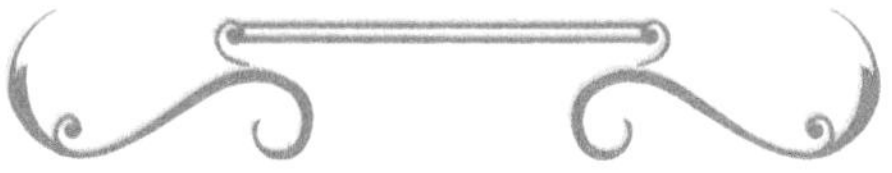

CHAPTER ONE:

Introducing Alistur the Magnificent

Alistur slowly guided the flowerpot higher and higher, up over his head. Pointing the tip of his birch wand toward the hovering object, he gently moved his wrist in circles, directing the pot to spin. "Slowly…slowly…" he whispered.

"Good morning Alistur!" Clara called out. Without an answer, she watched the planter waver in mid-air before it tilted sharply and crashed on the ground, grazing the hair on Alistur's head during its spiral downward.

With his concentration interrupted, Alistur cowered from the dirt and shrapnel spewing in every direction. Scrambling to his feet in embarrassment, he greeted her with a flushed face. "Morning, Miss Clara."

"I'm so sorry! It's my fault for startling you, Alistur! What brings you out so early today?" she asked, gaping at the mishap.

"Practicing my spells. Father says a young wizard can't practice enough." Alistur ran his fingers through the ginger-colored curls, shaking out small clods of dirt. "I'll be getting my crystal wand pretty soon, so I've got to be prepared."

"I see." Clara eyed him intently. "Well, it's going to be a beautiful day to practice."

Remembering his manners, Alistur tried his best to reciprocate the conversation. "And what about you, Miss Clara? Where are you going this morning?"

"To Saint Richarde. My students there have also been practicing very hard. I'm going to surprise them and spend some extra time helping to perfect their performances for the upcoming festival," she smiled. "And perhaps enjoy a couple of days of relaxation."

"Alistur! What was that commotion?" Thurlow pushed through the door, frowning at the mess strewn about. "Oh, good morning, Miss Clara!" Thurlow bowed, taking on a gentle tone when he noticed the music teacher standing nearby. "Please accept our apologies if Alistur frightened you with all of this."

"Not at all, Thurlow, I'm fine. I was just on my way to the coach. I'm off to Saint Richarde."

"I'm headed over to the castle now to meet with King Thorne, and the depot is right along the way. May I carry your bags for you?" he offered. "I see you have your hands full."

"That's very kind of you, Thurlow, but I can manage. It's just my instrument and a light bag. I'm only staying for a week, but thank you anyway." Clara nodded farewell. "Take care, Alistur."

"Have a nice trip, Miss Clara," Alistur mumbled, looking at the mess he would now have to clean up.

"Would you like to practice with me this morning, Father?"

"The king is waiting for me, Son." With a tousle of Alistur's hair, Thurlow side-stepped the broken pieces of the flowerpot, and dubiously bid his son a good day. "Oh, and try to stay out of trouble, eh? I've got my hands full the next couple of days." With a parting grin and a pat on his son's back, Thurlow headed toward the castle. "It's not long now until you receive your crystal wand! We'll have many opportunities to practice, Son!" he called over his shoulder.

"Of course, Father." Mustering a weak smile, Alistur attempted to conceal his disappointment.

Wiping sweat from the palms of his hands, Alistur's stomach stirred at the mention of his crystal wand. He had no idea what it would be like to traipse through the caverns in search of a crystal wand—or when it would take place—but according to his father, it would happen *soon*.

He'd only heard fragments of whispered conversations about other wizards' journeys into the depths of the crystal caverns. And those were comments shared between his father and grandfather, not intended for his ears. All he knows at this point is the fact that his father, his Grandfather Florian, and his Great-grandfather Balthazar, along with each and every wizard sworn to the Grimaldi Order since Balthazar's time, had trekked deep into the caverns to harvest their wands, and they'd been sworn to secrecy about their expeditions, making him all the more anxious. It's a tradition that had become a sacred rite of passage shared by all wizards who pledged to the Grimaldi teachings.

The Grimaldi wizards have served the Fleurbanian kings for centuries, and even though there are many other wizards throughout the Kingdom of Fleurbania, Alistur and his father, Thurlow, are the only remaining members of the Grimaldi lineage. At this point, Alistur was certain that his father would leave the earth without producing a sibling for him. Even though Thurlow rarely spoke of her, Alistur was intuitive enough to realize his father was still broken-hearted about his mother's death. Cynna was indeed the love of Thurlow's life, and when she died in childbirth with Alistur, Thurlow had never gotten over it. It would be up to Alistur to succeed his father in serving the kingdom, when the time comes—and to one day have a child of his own, to prepare him or her for the coveted role.

Many facets occupied young Alistur's tension-laced thoughts. At the forefront of his mind was the fact that in a matter of days or weeks—the timing was a mystery to him—he would make the journey of his lifetime to harvest a crystal wand.

Within an hour of waving goodbye to his father, Alistur had grown weary of practicing in the tedious confines of their small courtyard. He had the whole day to himself and he wanted a much more interesting place to perfect his craft. Lured by an irresistible temptation, he knew exactly where he would go. After a quick cleanup of the broken flower pot, Alistur's mood lifted as he closed the courtyard gate behind him and headed toward his awaiting audience.

After a brisk, ten-minute walk through the castle grounds, Alistur found the privacy he sought, deep within the royal gardens. It was a beautiful, warm morning on the second day of September, and the long, Fleurbanian summer was not yet over. Turning full circle to admire the beauty of the sanctuary, he was surrounded with an abundance of exciting possibilities. Scanning the grounds, Alistur's eyes took in the elaborate statuary centered in the main water fountain, reflecting pools, and freshwater streams flowing throughout the lush foliage. With the entire royal staff occupied with preparations for the upcoming festival, Alistur was certain he had the place all to himself—other than the resident animals roaming about, of course.

Standing in midst of the private haven, Alistur took center stage on a slab of stone, the maestro of all he surveyed. Focusing on a fat caterpillar inching its way across the nose of a life-sized ancient warrior of stone, he dramatically withdrew his birch wand from its sheath, feeling anxious about the idea of soon relinquishing his trusty wooden staff for a crystal one.

Needing a second volunteer to cast in his performance, along with the caterpillar, Alistur glanced over the plants and spied a praying mantis taking refuge on a leafy stem. Balancing on the frond, nearly invisible, the mantis stared back at him through bulging eyes.

"Ah ha! You cannot hide from Alistur the Magnificent!" he snickered. With a flick of his wrist and a snap of his cloak, he cast his spell upon the praying mantis, causing it to take a magical flight, landing on the nose of the warrior. Simultaneously, the caterpillar caught the edge of the frond, and dangled there by a few of its hind legs.

"A perfect switch!" he announced. Extremely proud of his choreography, Alistur took a bow to the imaginary cheers and applause from his make-believe audience.

Within minutes, other caterpillars as well as grasshoppers, crickets, and beetles were being juggled through the air—a fluttering symphony under his direction. Enticed by the wealth of opportunities throughout the gardens, Alistur soon became bored with the transformation of insects and set his sights on the swans and peacocks. Caught up in the audacious moment of his starring role, he decided to spice up his show with a little chant. Even though incantations weren't necessary to conduct his spells, he was certain it would make his performance more appealing.

"Strutting and swimming, beautiful birds of a feather, I shall ruffle those wings like a change in the weather!" he chanted.

Slicing his birch wand through the air, Alistur took aim toward the swans—planning to switch the white ones to black, and vice versa. But the moment he flared out his cloak in a flamboyant swirl, a gust of wind blew it up over his head, thwarting his dramatic intention. The peacocks strutting nearby shivered violently and then stood still, looking dazed. Suddenly void of their colorful plumage, some of them had transformed to stark albino while others had turned ebony. Thrusting their heads to the ground, they tried in vain to pick and peck at insects in the dirt. Startled by their own sounds, they made horrendous honking noises through obtrusive orange beaks. The swans, on the other hand, looked strangely beautiful as they glided across the water. Feathered in the dazzling colors of the peacocks, they proudly—but awkwardly—displayed magnificent plumes fanned out behind them.

"Uh-oh! What did I do to them?" His stomach churned as fear gripped his emotions. "Please, please, don't let them be injured!" he wailed.

Jolted by the sight, he thought of his father's words. Words he'd heard time after time: *"Never wield your powers aimlessly. Always take note of your surroundings and consider the presence of all elements…"*

"Never wield your powers aimlessly. Always take note of your surroundings and consider the presence of all elements..."

"Elements like the *wind*, for instance!" he scolded himself. Wringing his hands in despair, Alistur could only imagine his father's disappointment if he were to see this.

The unnatural-looking swans continued swimming, and the peacocks strutted off, unaware they were without their colorful plumes. Grateful the peculiar looking creatures didn't appear to be ailing, Alistur tried desperately to concentrate on what had gone wrong. But the longer he thought about it, the more confusing it became. How could he figure out how to reverse the spell if he didn't even know how the mistake had happened in the first place?

He reached for his Shield, wondering why it wasn't setting right the problems he was experiencing. Groping around his neck, his stomach pitched upside down when he realized the object he sought wasn't there. He'd forgotten to put his precious amulet around his neck that morning.

Birds fled from the bushes when he lashed out. "*Forgot* to wear my Shield?! The wizard's apprentice never forgets to wear his Shield!" he admonished himself.

Memories flooded his mind. Vividly, he recalled the excitement he felt on the day he'd received the Shield. A little more than a year ago, on his thirteenth birthday, the Grimaldi patriarch, his Great-grandfather Balthazar, had officiated the ceremony and proudly hung the family heirloom around his neck.

Engraved in his mind's eye, Alistur visualized the intricate details of the fox carved into the marble medallion. His Great-grandfather's words cycled through his mind "*...this Shield holds only temporary powers until you have harvested your crystal. Until that time, it may be used to reverse ill-fated, sincere mistakes. Always remember—just like the fox, this amulet protects one who will use all that he may possess of wisdom and wit in his own defense.*"

"Always remember–just like the fox, this amulet protects one who will use all that he may possess of wisdom and wit in his own defense."

Sadly, Alistur's ceremony was the last ritual Balthazar participated in. Not long after, he succumbed to ailing health, and passed peacefully in his slumber. Alistur had bonded with him over their frequent long talks, with Balthazar telling him stories about Thurlow as a young wizard. As long as he could remember, he'd always hoped that he would grow up to be just like his Great-grandfather Balthazar: a kind and wizened wizard. But right now, Alistur felt that aspiration slipping away.

Recollections of conversations echoed through his mind, reminding him of the importance of the achievement when he would be allowed to harvest a crystal wand. Just the way his Great-grandfather Balthazar, his Grandfather Florian, and his own father had done. It was the rite of passage that he'd been dreaming of. It was destined for him, and expected of him. And so far, he would be the last Grimaldi wizard to carry on the extraordinary family tradition.

Alistur recalled the promises he'd made when he took the oath and received the Shield. He'd promised to wield his powers under the very long list of commandments Balthazar had recited to him, and he'd promised never to use his powers for cruel pranks or with threatening intent—unless provoked by an opposing force. "That's hardly the case here," he thought, glaring at the horrific mix-up between the peacocks and swans, which had done nothing whatsoever to provoke him. "This definitely falls under the category of an ill-fated, sincere mistake," he assured himself while groping one more time for the Shield—hoping this time it might be hanging around his neck where it should be. It wasn't.

Shaken with humiliation at the mere thought of dishonoring his Great-grandfather, he now faced the worst predicament he'd ever been in. Speaking aloud to the birds, Alistur promised he would be back as soon as possible with his trusty Shield. He tucked the birch into its sheath and ran all the way home, with his cloak flapping wildly behind him.

When Alistur let himself in, he thanked the stars that his father was not home and would be occupied with the king for the entire day. He quickly grabbed his Shield from the small table in his bedroom and made a mad dash back to the royal gardens, hoping no one had noticed the awful situation he'd left behind.

Out of breath by the time he reached the gardens, Alistur let out a heavy sigh of relief to discover everything seemed fairly quiet and no one was there waiting to question him. The bland-looking peacocks were still preening and pecking at the ground—unaware of their lack of colorful plumage. The swans were still swimming—although not as gracefully as usual, given their new, tall feathers to which they were not accustomed.

While massaging the bumpy details of the Shield with his left hand, Alistur found the best vantage point for a clear view of the swans. Leveraging his knee over the arched back of a stone dragon, he steeled his nerves, and directed his wand toward the swans. With an enthusiastic flare of his cloak, he closed his eyes for a moment, anticipating everything would be rightfully restored when he opened them. Instead, flocks of small birds fluttered away as swarms of colorful dragonflies surged from the shrubs. Gaping at the sight, Alistur momentarily marveled at the oncoming throng heading directly at him. "Ouch!" he screamed as he attempted to swat them away. To his chagrin, the elegant dragonflies morphed into miniature fire-breathing beasts! Wincing in pain, he suddenly felt as though needles were pricking at the tips of his ears and all over his face. Slapping his hands about his head, he darted around aimlessly—until his shins smacked against the tail of the dragon, pitching him head over heels, and flipping the wand out of his hand. Grappling for his wand, Alistur continued crying out in pain—not so much from the scrapes on his bloody shins, but from the burning pangs of fire nipping at his head. Tiny flames squirted from the mouths of the dreadful pests, singeing his cloak and burning his skin with their efforts. Thankfully, his cloak offered modest protection, but his head remained exposed to the ongoing assault. Fighting off the attack, he scrambled on the ground, cowering under his cloak until the fiery swarm retreated.

Staggering to his feet in exhaustion, Alistur mostly regained his composure—with the exception of his face feeling like it were on fire. With no time to waste, he picked up his wand to continue his attempts at rectifying the situation, directing his attention this time toward the peacocks.

Once again, he wrapped his fingers around his trusty charm, closed his eyes, and repeated the actions. When Alistur opened his eyes, he couldn't believe what he saw. "Not again!" he yelled.

A few flamingos had been standing too close to the peacocks—which were apparently mingling near a zebra. Sure enough, they were also caught up in the cusp of his spell. The flamingos had taken on the zebra's black-and-white stripes!

"Why is this happening to me!?" he pleaded. Holding his head in his hands and tugging at his hair in frustration, Alistur paced around frantically.

Earlier that morning the gardens were a peaceful setting, full of elegant birds and exotic animals enjoying their pleasurable habitat. But now, in every direction, Alistur witnessed proof of his inexplicable failures.

Suddenly distracted by a familiar melody, Alistur crept toward the sound. Much to his dismay, Miss Clara was sitting in her favorite spot—atop the ledge surrounding the main fountain, strumming her lyre and singing to Princess Olivia's scruffy orange cat, Marigold.

With his arms stretched upward, Alistur pleaded to the clouds. ***"Why is she here?*** Miss Clara's supposed to be long gone on her way to Saint Richarde!" With fists clenched in rage, he continued his tirade.

"I can't concentrate with her annoying singing!" He quickly slapped his hand over his mouth, realizing he had spoken aloud.

Luckily, neither Clara nor the cat took interest in his direction. Dipping her outstretched paw into the basin, Marigold reached for a fat water bug. Watching the bug dart from harm's way, Clara smiled and sang louder, her beautiful voice resonating across the basin of the fountain.

Clara loved the way her voice carried over the water. Indeed, it sounded beautiful, and it was her favorite personal attribute. If truth were told, perhaps it was the only characteristic about herself she was proud of. But so far, her beautiful voice hadn't rewarded her with a happy life. Or any prospects for a husband.

She rested her lyre on the ledge to pet the cat. "Marigold, I'll be gone for a week, but we'll meet right here in our usual spot when I get back." Marigold purred in agreement, as Clara stroked her back. "My students are going to be so surprised to see me, and I like making them happy," she mused. "But, do you realize I'm almost *nineteen* years old?! What if this is all that's meant for me? Hmm? Is that why I'm feeling kind of sad, Marigold?" Marigold flopped onto her side and pawed at the strings on the lyre.

"I suppose it's complicated—but, why can't I be happier?" she asked. "Don't get me wrong, Marigold, I love being a music teacher, and I'm grateful for my blessings, and the good fortune to be living with Gemma and Giles. But…well, I long to spend my life with someone I truly care about—with all my heart. With someone who cares about *me* in the same way. *That* would make me happy!" Clara scratched Marigold's chin affectionately.

"Don't look at me like that, Marigold," she giggled. "I know *you* care for me." Marigold raised her head, eager for more scritches. "And I know Gemma and Giles care for me, too. But I'm talking about someone who wants to spend the rest of their days with me. *Only me.*" Clara looked at the woeful reflection staring back at her. "Is there someone out there for you, Clara?" she whispered into the water.

"Well, enough complaining, Marigold. I'd better go see if the coach is ready to leave."

Suddenly, a peculiar and distorted reflection appeared in the water, directly over her shoulder. When Clara turned around to get a better look, she let out a blood-curdling scream, and frantically scooped Marigold into her arms. Grappling with her lyre, and trying desperately to flee, Clara tripped over her suitcase, knocking it into the fast-moving stream, while pitching herself face-first into the water. And in the process, pulled Marigold in with her.

Whipping his wand through the air, aimed at the flamingos, Alistur lost his concentration, and spun around to see what Miss Clara was screaming about.

Stretching its neck over the basin of the fountain for a drink, with one leg tucked beneath its body, stood a zebra. With a flamingo-pink colored hide!

Alistur's stomach lurched. Glancing toward the stream a few yards away, he could see Miss Clara's lyre spinning circles in the swirling water, but she was nowhere in sight. His heart thudded against his chest, reminding him to breathe.

A short distance downstream, a large, strange-looking fish was causing quite a ruckus. It was flipping about aggressively, and making shrill, squeaking sounds. Curiously, it looked suspiciously like Marigold's head was connected to the body of the fluffy, orange fish. "Marigold? *Marigold!*" In a panic, Alistur wasn't sure whether to pluck the flailing creature out of the water or not. Paddling against the swirling current and struggling to keep her head above water, Marigold was being pulled by the rapid flow. Downstream she sailed, making the strange squeaking noises at the top of her lungs.

Wringing his hands in anguish, Alistur ran alongside the stream, desperately searching for Miss Clara. Bile rose to the back of his throat when he caught glimpse of her—part of her anyway. Clara was tangled in kelp, with her brown hair floating about her face, drifting with the current. The further downstream she went, the faster the current carried her.

"Miss Clara! *Please, come back!*" Alistur shrieked. Her hazel eyes were open wide, staring back at him with curiosity, while water flowed over her face. Her hand reached out to him—or was it the force of the current, moving her arm? Frantically, he ran alongside the stream, calling her name, to no avail. With bubbles trailing from her nostrils, and blood flowing from her forehead, Clara's limp body was swept into the dark stream—where it would empty into the depths of the Azlyn Sea.

Alistur's head throbbed with pulses of burning pain where the welts had swollen on his face and ears. But those wounds, and the pain they caused, were the least of his worries. Realizing his pleading was futile, Alistur sank to his knees, overwrought with shame for causing this calamity, but more so, with guilt for not being able to rescue Miss Clara. Biting his lip until it bled, he could not hold back his tears. "What did I do? *Oh, what did I do?*" he scolded himself through clenched teeth. "The birds are one thing…but…*Miss Clara!?*" he spewed through his trembling lips.

Growing more paranoid with each passing second, Alistur knew Princess Olivia could be along any moment, and he didn't want to be caught anywhere near the area—especially if she was looking for Marigold. He had to get out of there, and fast. The Rabbit Hole was the only thought that came to mind, even though he knew it was forbidden to use. His father had taken him through the secret passage a few times, and told him it was intended only for shepherding members of the royal family to safety during life-threatening circumstances, or to be used as an expedient route should he and his father need to reach the castle without being seen. In his hysteria, Alistur easily convinced himself that this was one of those justifiable moments. And besides, the shortcut would get him home quickly. He ran to the far corner of the gardens where the entrance to the passage was hidden. Taking one last look around, Alistur hoped with all his being that no one would notice the mishaps before he could return with a plan to rectify everything. He parted the weeds from around the secluded steps, and crept down the four crumbling stairs.

The base of the short staircase dead-ended into a solid rock wall. The cleverly disguised access to the Rabbit Hole gave the pretense it was merely the ruins of an ancient wall—an illusion reinforced by its covering of dead, tangled vines. Pushing his hands through the gnarly, dried shrubbery, Alistur felt along the wall for the opening. Slipping behind the dusty entanglement, he shimmied his way into the crevice. Inside the crevice, the walls forced an immediate sharp turn, allowing only a small amount of space to maneuver the corner. Flattened against the wall and feeling claustrophobic, Alistur sucked in his breath to make the next move. Closing his eyes, he recalled the last time he had followed his father through the tunnel. It had seemed easy back then, with his father guiding him along, but this time he felt paralyzed without a torch to light his way. He was trapped in the darkness and gasping for air, as panic washed over him. Gritting his teeth, with sweat trickling from his temples, he silently prayed for the strength to clear his head so he could visualize the next move he needed to make. Just one more sharp turn. Forcing his body to move along the wall, he willed himself to inch his way around the last corner. Finally sensing open space around him, he stopped to calibrate his direction.

Continuing at a slow pace through pitch darkness, Alistur worked his way through the passage, fighting off spiderwebs that he couldn't see. Exhausted from the ordeal and his equilibrium out of kilter, he tripped over a rock. Unable to keep his balance, he fell to the ground, skinning the palms of his hands and causing further damage to his already battered knees and cloak. The tunnel was narrow enough to reach out and touch both sides—evidenced by his bleeding fingertips from scraping along the jagged walls. Every few yards he flinched at the flutter of starlings being provoked from their roosts. Alistur had never been in the Rabbit Hole by himself and he hated being in it alone.

After a few harrowing minutes of stumbling through darkness, he finally came to the end of the passage. Running his hands across the wall in front of him, he felt around for the outline of the doorway. Tracing the crack, he pushed against it. It didn't move. Bracing his shoulder against the door, he shoved harder. Still nothing, the door wouldn't budge. He shuddered at the thought of turning around and having to backtrack all the way through the tunnel, back to the gardens. Forcing that thought from his mind, he braced himself against the resistance of the door. Grunting and shoving with every ounce of strength he had, the thick door finally gave way and swung open into Thurlow's laboratory.

Once inside, Alistur took a look at his face in the reflecting glass. Wincing at his image, he stared at the welts on his face that stung profusely— they looked as bad as they actually felt. He pilfered through shelves of apothecary jars and containers of all shapes and sizes until he found the medicine he was looking for. The ointment he selected soothed the hot spots momentarily, but it did little for their unsightly appearance.

Not quite sure how he would explain the swollen bumps on his face, Alistur headed to his bedroom. He needed time to think before facing his father. He quickly removed his tattered cloak and burrowed beneath the blankets on his bed, relishing the temporary relief he felt at the distance between him and his bad decisions. Physically and mentally exhausted, he was distraught with the myriad emotions cluttering the forefront of his mind, and ashamed of his hapless actions in the royal gardens. The mix-up with the animals was one thing, but his shame was nothing compared to the guilt that consumed him about Miss Clara. He couldn't block the look on her face from his mind's eye. The hairs rose at the nape of his neck as the vision flashed before him. He was certain Miss Clara had actually ***looked at him and reached for him*** before she was swept away. He shivered at the thought, unable to comprehend exactly what had happened to her. Because it occurred by his own hand during a misguided spell, he believed in his heart there would surely be a way to bring her back.

ᔓᔕ

The house was still when Thurlow arrived home less than two hours later.

"Alistur?" Thurlow called, making his way toward his son's room. "What are you doing in bed already? Let's have some supper and you can tell me about your day." No response. Thurlow stepped closer to the side of his bed. "Alistur? Are you well?"

Feigning sleep, Alistur barely stirred under the covers, as another wave of shame and guilt washed over him. In a groggy voice, as if he'd been long asleep, he did his best to convince his father to leave him be. "Sorry, Father, I'm not feeling very well. I'd better stay in bed."

"I'll put on some broth and I'm sure you'll feel better once you've eaten," Thurlow suggested.

A burning thickness formed in Alistur's throat, stifling his voice as he hunched closer to the wall. "Thank you anyway, Father, but I'm not hungry."

"Alright, Son. I'll keep a kettle on the stove in case you feel like having some tea later."

Despite his exhaustion, Alistur was too restless to sleep. While thrashing about, his father's sage advice echoed louder and louder between his ears: "... *Always take note of your surroundings and consider the presence of all elements...*" The excitement he had felt that morning when he entered the royal gardens to practice had turned into a dismal string of catastrophic failures.

"Why did I have to go and do all of this? And so close before getting my crystal wand?" he grumbled into his pillow, expecting his father would, any day now, announce that it was time to make the trek to the caverns. He'd been fantasizing what that day would be like. Thinking about the ritual was mind-boggling, even though under any other circumstances, it was a ritual he could hardly wait to participate in. But now, he worried that his father would announce it was time to make the trek before he'd had the opportunity to correct his colossal mishaps. He pounded his pillow at the thought of his father canceling the trek. "That's just what I deserve!" he chastised himself. Pulling his blanket over his head, he prayed his father hadn't heard him scolding himself.

Alistur stayed awake until he heard the familiar sounds of Thurlow's snoring. Satisfied that his father was fast asleep, he quietly slipped out of bed and donned his tattered cloak. Armed with his Shield, trusty birch wand, and a fierce determination to fix his mistakes, he ran all the way to the royal gardens with a torch flame streaking through the darkness behind him.

The gardens were eerily quiet, other than the repetitive songs of the crickets and trickles of water moving through the stream. The moon shone brightly across the calm pond, without as much as a ripple. The swans were nowhere in sight. Looking around for the peacocks and the zebra, Alistur's midnight safari was uneventful so far. "Where *are* they? Please, please, let them all be alright," he whispered. "Switching feathers is one thing, but I'll never forgive myself if…if…" he shuddered at the thought of causing harm to Miss Clara.

Tiptoeing over to Clara's favorite spot at the fountain, Alistur leaned over the basin, holding tightly to the torch. Looking at his pitiful, welt-covered reflection in the water, he felt nothing but despair. "Poor Miss Clara. *Where are you?*" he muttered. The distorted face looking back at him projected more guilt for practicing his spells while she was in the area that morning.

Alistur sat on the ground to think. Within seconds, the silence was broken as voices intruded his thoughts. ***"Now what!?"*** he muttered. Straining to hear, he sat motionless, as the voices grew louder. Guests were leaving the castle. He could hear the steward showing them out, but they didn't leave. They kept hanging around with ceaseless laughter and idle conversations.

Alistur couldn't risk being seen. He was trapped, with only the one way out. Feeling defeated, he headed straight for the Rabbit Hole.

Holding the torch low, he parted the vines to locate the steps and quickly inched his way into the crevice. As bad as being in the tunnel had been earlier that day, he didn't like it any better having the torch to guide his way. *Especially* with the torch. This time he could see just how creepy it was. Slashing at the spiderwebs with the flame, he saw bats catching insects in mid-air, and a few mice fleeing from the intrusive blaze. Noticing all the things he couldn't see earlier got the best of him and he couldn't take it a second longer. He forged his way through the maze of turns, and ran all the way to the other end of the tunnel. Gasping for air by the time he reached the door to the laboratory, he doused the torch and braced himself to push. Already loosened from earlier, the heavy door gave way instantly. The momentum forced him to the ground, slapping his hands hard on the stone floor.

He lay still for a moment, rubbing his stinging palms and listening for any sign that his father might have awakened. Satisfied that Thurlow was still snoozing peacefully, Alistur pulled himself to his feet and crept through the house to his bedroom.

It wasn't until he took off his clothing to get back in bed that he realized his Shield was not hanging around his neck—*again!* Rifling through the heap of clothes on the floor turned up nothing. Alistur sat on the edge of his bed and rubbed his head with his fists. Retracing his steps in his mind, he tried in vain to remember the last time he had touched the Shield. Nothing came to mind.

In despair, he crawled under the covers and fretted about all that had happened that day, and tried to figure out how he would tell his father about it.

After spending an agonizing hour trying to get to sleep, Alistur tiptoed into the laboratory, in search of answers.

CHAPTER TWO:

Aristocracy Under the Sea

Clara opened and closed her eyes as she bobbed along the jagged coastline. Being carried along with the currents of the Azlyn Sea, she drifted in and out of consciousness, unable to escape the mind-boggling turbulence.

Eventually, her body came to rest. Feeling strangely comfortable, she relaxed in powerful, caring arms. Rocking to and fro in rhythm with the waves, she was lulled back to sleep ever so gently each time she raised her head—unaware she was actually being cradled and protected from drifting too close to the sharp reefs.

As the minutes passed she started to regain her senses little by little, but felt constricted each time she tried to raise her arms. They felt heavy and it was too much effort for her to lift them. Clara sensed something enveloping her body, but was unable to break through the lethargic haze clouding her mind. With her eyes still closed, she labored to peel slimy shreds of kelp from her face and pushed thick, gooey fronds away from her body. Over and over, in a foggy state of mind, she repeated the chore. The fronds clinging to her were getting heavier and becoming more difficult to pull away. Quickly exhausted from her labors, she dozed a bit longer before stirring again.

When she opened her eyes once again, Clara was overcome with nausea. Peeking cautiously, she shuddered at the images before her. Jellyfish danced about in front of her; bobbing up and down, darting sideways, and back and forth. At first glance there were two, then they multiplied, almost in time with the new wave of nausea that overtook her. They were translucent and much too difficult to focus on. Painfully disoriented, she closed her eyes and worked in slow motion, still trying to escape the tangled mass embracing her. Gradually, she was able to open her eyes and hold them open, which only made her more aware of the throbbing pain in her head and the sickening feeling in her stomach. Among the tangle of kelp, slimy *arms* seemed to be everywhere—not fronds, like she thought. One by one, she tried pushing them away. Each time she made progress, another appendage would reach out and drag her back. Clara squirmed and fought in vain, trying to free herself of what she hoped was all a bad dream. But it wasn't; the pain in her head told her it was all too real.

Confused about her surroundings, she tried to focus on where she might be. The confusion turned into frustration. She simply could not make sense of her whereabouts, or even comprehend where she was *supposed* to be. Absolutely nothing seemed right and she had no concept of how she'd gotten where she was.

After struggling for what seemed like hours in a stupor, she found herself looking face-to-face into dark beady eyes. The giant octopus stared back, gently cradling her in its strong arms. Suddenly conscious of the fact she was under water, Clara instinctively held her breath and kicked at her captor with all her might. Her efforts were futile, which only caused the pulsating pain in her head to intensify. One by one, the giant mollusk released its suction-bearing arms. In a panic, Clara swam away, clueless of which direction to go, searching in vain for the surface. Disoriented, she swam frantically in circles, looking for a hint of light, until she could no longer hold her breath. Feeling as though her lungs would explode, she gave in to the pain and gasped for air. Immediately, the discomfort in her lungs subsided. Bewildered by the fact she was still alive, she was utterly confused to realize she had not drowned, but instead, was breathing perfectly fine under the water.

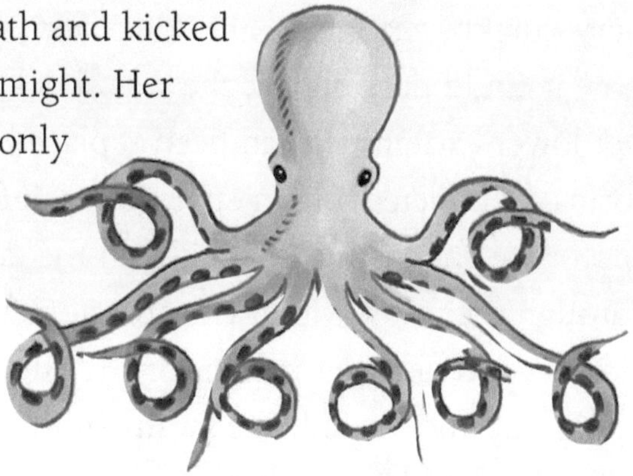

Other than the very sore bump on her forehead, she started to feel somewhat better, and her nausea had subsided. Reaching up to touch her forehead, traces of blood flowed in front of her face as jagged memories passed through her mind. In a fleeting moment of clarity, she recalled the fact she'd been playing her lyre and looked around for the instrument, to no avail. Fragmented memories hovered just outside the perimeter of her comprehension and then faded. Struggling to think clearly through the fogginess in her head, an image of Gemma and Giles passed through her mind's eye, but she was unable to make sense of it.

Very quickly, she made other discoveries. Unable to fathom how it could possibly be, she was shocked and amazed that her lower extremities had been replaced with a shapely, scaled form—complete with an enormous tail fin. In sheer panic at the discovery, she instinctively flipped the tail, projecting herself through the water with awkward momentum. The transformation was beyond her comprehension. Trying to flee from what she could not understand, she swam around aimlessly.

The curious octopus glided along behind her for several minutes, navigating every move she made. Eventually, it lost interest and meandered away when Clara took refuge behind giant reefs.

~

With their nets heavy from a successful abalone harvest, Treena and Delpha swam toward the cove. Nearing the reefs, they noticed an unfamiliar lone sea maiden flitting about, treading water in large circles above the surface. Keeping their distance, they observed her odd behavior for a couple of minutes, then slowly swam a bit closer, dragging their bulky nets behind.

When Clara spotted the two maidens, she quickly crossed her arms over her body trying to cover herself, as her transformation and loss of clothing was an embarrassing mystery she could not grasp.

Treena and Delpha swam a bit closer. "Do you need help?" Treena asked. "Are you looking for something?"

Clara hesitated, not sure whether to answer. *If I'm dreaming, then it won't be necessary to answer,* she thought. But Treena's voice sounded so real, and very kind—and Clara really did need help, so she responded. "I'm looking for my lyre…and my clothing…I guess." Blushing, she averted her eyes, wondering why they, too, didn't try to cover themselves.

"Your *lyre?"* they asked in unison with curious looks on their faces.

"Yes. I was just playing it at the fountain…where I always sing… while waiting for the coach. But…but it was delayed." Her voice trailed off as she held her hand to her throbbing forehead, trying to recall what had happened. "I was on my way to Saint Richarde, but then…."

"The coach?" Delpha mused. "To Saint Richarde?"

"Yes. I really must find my lyre. I—I'm just so confused, and my students…my music students are there…" Trying very hard not to cry, Clara held her quivering lip in place with her teeth. It seemed as though she were slipping in and out of a puzzling dream. She thought she was awake while talking with the two sea maidens, but it seemed surreal and not right at all.

"Please, don't cry. We'll help you. I promise we will. I'm Treena, and this is Delpha. What's your name?"

"Clara."

"You're hurt, Clara." Treena held out her hand. "Come with us."

"Where?" Clara asked meekly. "Where are we going?"

"To the cove," Treena answered. "The rest of our tribe is not far—Goldfin Cove is just north of here."

"Where's *your* tribe?" Delpha asked.

Clara looked dumbfounded. "I live with Gemma and Giles."

"There are just three of you in your tribe?" Delpha asked with a quizzical look.

"Yes. Um, no! I don't have a *tribe*. They are just people—like me."

"People? *You live with people?"* Delpha looked very confused.

"Yes, of course…I live with the Renwicke's. At Mont Renault." Clara was having a very difficult time explaining herself.

Treena attempted to clear the confusion. "Where are your people now?"

"I'm not sure." Clara reached up to caress the bump on her forehead.

"King Stern will help you. We can also tend to your wounds," Treena assured her.

"King Stern?" The name didn't sound familiar to Clara at all.

"Yes, he's the king of our tribe—the Alecians," Delpha interjected. "He may even know of your *people*…Gemma and Giles." Even though Clara didn't see it, Delpha's face lit up talking about King Stern, but she could sense Delpha was quite proud of him nonetheless.

"The Alecians?" Clara mumbled.

"Yes, come with us. You're just in time to be our guest for dinner." Treena smiled and shook her net stuffed full of abalone.

"Will others be there?" Clara asked, observing their bulging nets.

"Yes, of course. Our whole tribe is there waiting for us," Delpha asserted.

Suddenly, Clara became intrigued with her hair floating about. Somehow her straggly brown hair had become volumes of vibrant, chestnut colored tresses, now cascading to her waist. Curiously, Treena and Delpha watched as Clara examined handfuls of her hair—as though she were seeing it for the first time.

Clara regarded the other two briefly while she examined her own strands. Treena's hair was raven, with a subtle bluish tone glimmering in the sunlight. The mass of waves looked stunning against the opaque, molasses hue of her smooth skin. For a fleeting moment she looked into Treena's eyes, but not long enough to determine whether they were blue or lavender.

Delpha also looked exquisite. Heaps of platinum hair tumbled about—a near match to her dazzling alabaster colored flesh. Delpha's icy grey eyes looked back at her impatiently.

"Are you ready to meet our tribe?" Treena coaxed.

"I can't go like this!" Clara tried to cover up again.

"Like what?" they both asked.

Trying to gain clarity through her fogginess, Clara wondered why the other two showed no concern at all for their bareness. "Treena, may I have a piece of your net?"

With a curious look, Treena emptied part of her abalone into Delpha's net, then took her dagger from the sheath at her waist and cut off a wide strip from the top of the net. "How's this?"

Clara reached for the dagger. "May I?"

Eyeing Clara suspiciously, Delpha glowered at the extra weight added to her already heavy haul and watched cautiously as Treena handed over her weapon along with the piece of net.

"Thank you." Clara grasped the handle of the dagger. Without any previous experience handling such a weapon, she awkwardly cut a jagged slit in the center of the net and slipped the opening over her head. She then plucked handfuls of sea grass and wove the strands through the holes. "I think I'm ready now."

Treena eagerly took possession of her dagger and grinned at the unusual garment Clara had crafted. "Let's get going. We'll take a look at that cut on your forehead as soon as we get to the palace."

"The *palace?"* Again, Clara looked confused.

Delpha looked at her in amazement. "Yes, Aquan's Palace! King Stern is a direct descendant of Aquan."

"Aquan?" Clara had no idea whatsoever who or what Delpha was talking about.

"You've never heard of Aquan?" Delpha was astonished.

Sensing a disparaging tone in Delpha's voice, Clara looked at her timidly. "No, I'm sorry. But please, lead the way," she answered.

Delpha dove under the surface, and veered away from the shoreline quickly gaining speed, while Treena stayed behind with Clara to make sure she could keep up.

Within seconds, Clara was also gliding through the water with ease and gaining incredible speed, easily keeping pace with the other two. As they swam, Clara began to feel better. Enchanted by the beauty of the underwater world, her senses were in tune to the intricacies of the sea, and her headache diminished. They dodged jellyfish and eels, while schools of brightly colored fish darted away just in time. Along the way, Clara marveled at the size of giant sea horses, and turtles meandering along, before they navigated through a forest of kelp.

As they neared the cove, the water felt warmer. Soon, Clara noticed that several very large and very unusual-looking sea creatures had joined them, seemingly leading the way. The rotund mammals were being propelled through the water by thick, paddle-shaped fins protruding from their sides. The enormous creatures had large round heads with flat, turned up snouts. They occasionally shot high above the surface and dove back down, playfully escorting the sea maidens around the bend into a beautiful lagoon.

Well into the lagoon, the sea maidens broke surface and Treena explained that the giant sea creatures were friendly. "Don't be frightened," Treena said. "They're sea oxen, and they're very helpful to us. You'll see." Winding their way further through the lagoon, they came upon two massive doors rising from below the surface. Sprawled across the double doors was an elaborate carving of an octopus, spanning at least twenty feet in width across the doors. Surveying the intricate features, a sense of familiarity washed over her, as Clara stared into the dark, round eyes of the effigy.

"What's the matter?" Delpha asked.

"Nothing. I just…nothing. I'm fine."

"Don't be frightened. We call him Lord Regalion—a rendition of our friendly protector," Treena explained. "Let's go in."

"Protector," Clara mused. "That's good…that's very good to know." She refrained from mentioning her personal encounter with an octopus earlier that day.

Treading water in front of the doors, Treena pulled out a large seashell from a netted bag tied at her waist and blew a signal through the conch.

Within seconds, the giant doors parted, allowing the maidens entrance into the ruins of the half-sunken palace. Just inside the vestibule, the water receded to low levels, swirling throughout toppled architecture. Slowly treading water and turning around in all directions, Clara was speechless.

Swimming further into the great foyer, she felt a strong vibration swooshing behind her. She whirled around to see twelve of the giant sea oxen move into alignment at the doors, with six positioned along each door. The oxen dove below the surface and pushed their snouts through large rings linked to massive chains that were secured along the edges of each door. The creatures tugged on the chains and the doors began moving. Perfectly orchestrated, the doors drew together. Enormous bolts clanked in place as the powerful teams passed each other in synchronized formation. Once the doors were secure, the oxen dropped the chains and surfaced at the far side of the foyer where other sea maidens were waiting with treats of mackerel. Defying their hefty bodies, the oxen shot up out of the water, easily catching their rewards in mid-air.

Adjacent to each side of the doors, stone walls jutted down into the floor of the lagoon, and rose high above the surface, enclosing them inside a magnificent fortified domain.

When she finally spoke, Clara's whisper resonated over the water with a melodious sound. "This is exquisite."

"Yes, of course it is—you'd be a fool not to love it!" Delpha boasted.

The spacious and ornate appearance of the architecture reminded Clara of the one and only other luxurious property she'd ever been in—King Thorne's castle at Mont Renault. She was starting to recall other bits and pieces, and she thought about the quarters she had occupied on the castle grounds with the royal composers, Gemma and Giles. Fragments were slowly coming together. Once again, she recalled sitting at the edge of the fountain playing her lyre and singing to Marigold. "Yes…oh yes, ***I love to sing!"*** She blurted, earning odd looks from Treena and Delpha.

Treena led her to an area of the palace where the water was especially shallow. Reclining marble slabs were scattered throughout tall sea grasses, and colorful, blooming plants grew in abundance. Treena directed her to a comfortable spot, practically hidden among a dense cluster of sweet-smelling foliage. "Here, you just lie back while I tend to the cut on your forehead," Treena cooed.

With a flip of her strong tailfin, Clara easily hoisted herself onto the reclining slab. Feeling sleepy, she barely noticed Treena treating her wound with a sticky substance, then covering it with a piece of kelp.

"You can rest here. We'll come back and get you when dinner is ready." Treena smiled sweetly and left her alone.

Infiltrated with pure oxygen from the abundance of plants, the pleasant area felt wonderfully therapeutic. Lulled by the feel of tepid water lapping over her, Clara quickly dozed off, but her sleep was muddled with sad realizations. She dreamt of her hard-working father losing his life six years ago in a horrific storm at sea. At the time, he was employed by King Thorne as a fisherman. The king took responsibility for the tragedy, and had provided work for her mother in his court. Although her mother had been grateful to the king for his kindness and for giving her the means to support her only child, it pained Clara deeply to know her mother had spent the last four years of her life grieving the loss of her husband, while toiling away to support her. Clara truly believed her mother had slowly died of a broken heart. Her parents had worked hard to give her a good life, but Clara's happy childhood had been taken from her when she was only twelve years old, leaving her with her own broken heart.

While she dreamt, conjured memories reinforced the fact that she was basically alone in the world, longing for someone to love her—not the same kind of love and caring she received from Gemma and Giles after her mother died. The two composers had gotten to know Clara while she helped her mother work around Mont Renault. Without children of their own, the couple became quite fond of her. They had recognized her brilliant musical ability while listening to her sing as she worked alongside her mother. When her mother died, they welcomed Clara into their home and furthered her musical inclinations by establishing her as a music teacher for the students of Mont Renault and surrounding villages. Clara would always be grateful to them for taking her in, but deep in her heart she knew that something—or someone—was missing in her life.

Her existence before this transformation continued passing through her mind's eye in the form of vivid dreams.

"Clara? Clara?" Her eyes flew open to see Treena staring directly into her face.

"Oh, I'm sorry." Clara stifled a yawn. "I was…I was in deep thought."

"Deep thought? You were sound asleep! I brought King Stern by to meet you, but you were sleeping so soundly we didn't want to disturb you. I hate to wake you now, but I know you must be famished, and dinner is ready." Treena helped her slide off of the reclining slab.

"Follow me." Treena led her through a labyrinth of long, half-submerged hallways. Through the tiny canals, they passed ornate sculptures, and arched niches holding marble statues. Oddly, the statues were stylishly draped in chains of gold and exquisite ropes of pearls. The passageways were remarkably well lit with numerous torches and oil lanterns mounted above the surface of the water. The torches cast colorful yet distorted shadows through the channels and onto the murals painted on the drab stone walls.

When Clara entered the grand dining room, she was awe-stricken by the bold statements of extravagance everywhere she looked. An enormous round table protruding above the water was laden with an abundance of delicacies, all beautifully displayed on silver and golden platters.

Beyond a long row of columns and arches, the dining room opened to a secluded alcove. An alluring sanctuary filled the space between the exterior palace walls and the cliff side of the surrounding lagoon.

"This really is a palace!" Clara marveled at the exquisite domain. "I had no idea anything could be this beautiful!"

Delpha pursed her lips. "Of course it's beautiful—it's a palace. Just like I told you," lacing her comment with a slight tone of arrogance.

Treena shot a terse look at Delpha for speaking to their guest with an indignant tone.

Clara ignored the comment and squinted her eyes, looking toward the view beyond the dining area. "How is it that the cliff walls are emanating sparkles from *within* the rock?"

"Please, take this slab, so King Stern can tell you all about it." Treena urged Clara to take Delpha's regular spot right next to the king. Clara eagerly hoisted herself onto the slab, missing the angry pout Delpha directed toward Treena.

King Stern, however, did not miss Delpha's icy glare. He chose not to address her demeanor in front of the others, but he realized Delpha's petulant gestures were becoming more frequent.

"Welcome to our feast, Clara." King Stern waved his hand toward the abundance of food before them. "To answer your question, the cliff walls are richly embedded with layers of minerals and veins of precious gems running throughout. As you can see, the view is all the more captivating when illuminated by the stars or the sun." While he spoke, the king watched with amusement as Clara nervously tried to weave stray grasses back into the covering she'd fashioned earlier. "Under the influence of a starlit night and a full moon, such as we have tonight, *everything* is dazzling."

Before the lavish meal began, Treena introduced Clara to those around the table, but there were too many names for her to remember. Large gatherings and small talk were not among her most comfortable elements. *All of the merfolk look fantastic,* she thought. And all of them aglow with an unusual, opaque quality to their flawless skin, with absolute masses of gorgeous hair. Noticing all of the fancy jewels worn by everyone at the table, Clara felt quite inferior garbed only in the grass-covered netting. She was unsure whether the tribe had dressed up for this specific meal, or whether they always wore such fanciful adornments. She hadn't noticed Treena or Delpha wearing such jewelry when they had first met, but at the time her mind was quite foggy, and besides, she'd tried not to observe that much about their bodies.

From the very moment King Stern engaged her in conversation, he had captivated Clara's undivided attention. Perhaps it was his knowledge about the history of the palace—or simply the way he looked into her eyes when he spoke. His eyes sparkled as he enlightened her about life in their exciting kingdom. It was as if *she* mattered. He shared every detail, and she wanted to absorb every word he uttered. At times she felt like they were the only two at the table.

Mutually, Clara had captivated King Stern's attention in much the same way.

Soon, Delpha had witnessed quite enough of their chatting. Feeling left out, she suddenly tried to redirect the conversation. "Stern, Clara probably has no interest about our ancient history! Especially those tiresome old stories about the Brueland pirates." The comment earned her a cross look from King Stern.

"Oh, Delpha, it's really quite alright! I truly do want to hear *everything,*" Clara insisted, sensing the possessiveness Delpha exhibited for King Stern.

Clara was slowly gathering more fragmented memories and piecing together her previous life at Mont Renault. However, she struggled with her comprehension of time—not able to discern the fact it was only earlier that morning when she'd fallen into the stream.

The stories King Stern told sounded vaguely familiar and she was eager to hear more. Similarly, her appetite was insatiable. While she devoured abalone, oysters, and sea fronds, Clara hung on every last detail crossing King Stern's lips.

Stern continued educating her about the old northern country formerly known as Brueland. "During the invasion, and many times thereafter, the palace was plundered and badly damaged by canon fire from pirate ships, eventually causing these sections to topple into the sea. Later, when the pirates' stronghold in the lagoon was crushed and buried, their fortunes of heisted loot became hostage to the tides, settling where they may under the sea. When the treasure chests come adrift, they settle right here in this very cove."

The more the king talked, Clara started remembering what she had previously known about the old, grisly country. The savage pirates of Brueland had been arch enemies of the Kingdom of Fleurbania for more than a century. After the Bruelanders were finally defeated by Queen Ruthelda's loyal army, the entire country of Brueland was absorbed by Fleurbania. Of course, it had been impossible over the years to extinguish the rogue bands of pirates still marauding the coast, even after the downfall of Brueland.

"Tell me, Clara, how do you like our dwelling?" Stern gazed about, drawing attention to the expanse of the ruins.

Before Clara could answer, Delpha interjected again. "As you can see, *we're* the most elite tribe in all of the Azlyn Sea!" Laden with diamonds on most of her fingers, she fussed with layers of pearls and necklaces encrusted with more diamonds hanging from her slender neck. The attention Delpha brought to herself earned another hard look from the king, but it didn't deter her in the least. "Sometimes the jewels simply float up from the ruins below. Like *gifts* sent to us from ghosts of the pirates," Delpha proclaimed, ignoring King Stern.

Unable to break her stare, Clara couldn't take her eyes off of Delpha. She was consumed by Delpha's goddess-like beauty: a vision of platinum, garbed in glittering diamonds.

"…the jewels simply float up from below?" Clara mused.

Stern intercepted Delpha's attempt to draw more attention to herself, and turned once again toward Clara. "Like I was describing before, while ancient shipwrecks are rotting away, the treasure chests are released to the sea, and eventually carried by the tide, until they settle here in the cove." Stern paused a moment while Clara digested the explanation. "Many of the chests are damaged and rotted. So, when we are moving them into the confines of the palace, some of the treasures fall back to the floor of the lagoon, only to be unearthed by the undercurrents—in time, swept into the canals of the palace."

Intrigued by Stern's explanation, Clara shook her head in acknowledgement. "That certainly explains why your tribe is so well-adorned," she smiled as she looked about the table, focusing on the finery worn by the merfolk.

Soon the dinner conversation turned to sharing stories about the treasure hunters and fishermen who relentlessly hunt the merfolk. Outwardly frightened by these accounts, Clara looked to Stern for confirmation as to what was being said.

"I'm afraid it's true." King Stern's voice took on an edge. "Even though Goldfin Cove is no longer a stronghold for plundering pirates, it doesn't stop others from trying to capture us—in hopes of being led to the riches."

Between hushed comments and whispers among each other, the merfolk around the table seemed curious as to how any maiden in the Azlyn Sea did not know about their tribe, or how they'd come to occupy the palace ruins. However, seeing how their king was enamored with the pretty guest, they did everything possible to make her feel welcome. All of them except for Delpha. She rolled her eyes and quietly scoffed at the many facts Clara seemed unknowledgeable about.

When the last morsel was taken from a silver platter before her, Clara noticed her reflection on the edge of the tray. Curiously, she tilted the gleaming silver toward her face. Somehow, she looked the same—yet astonishingly different at the same time. Those were certainly her hazel eyes looking back at her, but her skin looked thicker, like a cream-colored velvet—with the exception of the ghastly green piece of kelp plastered across the cut on her forehead. Looking beyond the bandage though, something stirred inside her. The smattering of freckles across her nose was gone. And, like she'd noticed earlier, her mousy, drab hair had been replaced with volumes of wavy, vibrant, chestnut-colored tresses. Tilting the silver tray back and forth, she saw radiance. And for the first time ever, she experienced a moment of confidence in how she perceived herself. She actually felt *beautiful.*

Delpha seized the opportunity to niggle at Clara one more time. "Poor Clara, you look utterly exhausted." With her slender fingers heavy with jewels, she swept her locks to one side. "Undoubtedly, you must be ready for a good night's sleep."

"Yes, I am a bit tired, and I must look a mess." Feeling embarrassed again, Clara ran her fingers along the bandage on her forehead and poked wilted grasses back in place that had strayed from the tattered net bodice.

"Don't worry. We can fit you with a brand-new piece of netting tomorrow!" With too much sweetness in her voice, Delpha giggled.

No one else dared to comment on her veiled criticism of their guest.

Treena noticed the embarrassment Clara felt, and came to her defense. "Come with me, Clara. I'll show you to your chambers." Clara slid away from the table and followed Treena.

As Clara departed, the king's strong, soothing voice echoed behind her. "Tomorrow I'll take you on a grand tour of the rest of the palace, Clara. Until then, sweet dreams!" She looked back to acknowledge his parting words with a warm smile.

Again, Clara was astounded at the size and opulence of the chamber Treena led her to. "All of this?" she marveled. "Just for me?"

"Absolutely! The palace has many rooms. How does this one suit you?" Treena clasped her hands.

"I…I love it." Clara whispered. "I can sleep right under the stars," she noted, gazing upward, through the open ceiling. The spacious chamber was indeed exquisite. From the light of the full moon and the stars, the shallow water rippled with brilliant reflections, as colorful fish darted in and out of willowy sea grasses throughout the chamber.

"Yes, and if you look in that direction, you have a splendid view of Pearlcliff." Treena waved toward the breathtaking view.

Clara wasted no time getting comfortable on a sloped marble slab, supported by two ornate columns, and submerged halfway in the water.

Treena lit an oil torchiere near the slab. "It's a good idea to have extra light until you are accustomed to the surroundings," she advised.

"Good night, Treena." Clara searched for the words to express her gratitude, but found none worthy. "Thank you…for everything."

"You're welcome, Clara. Rest well. It sounds like King Stern has a busy day planned for you tomorrow."

Clara was exhausted, yet she didn't want sleep to come. She lay there, looking at the stars, and absorbing the beauty and comfort of her surroundings. *Comfort.* She couldn't remember a time when she'd ever felt more comfortable, as water gently lapped across the marble she rested upon. Not only comfortable, she also felt safe and secure. And at peace. For reasons she couldn't explain, she felt like she *belonged* with the Alecians. A single tear of joy slid down her cheek as she fought to think through the fogginess still clouding her mind, trying to make sense of everything. Finally, she closed her eyes, and relinquished herself to the serendipity of her transformation.

ᔓ

When Treena returned to the dining table, the conversations were still going strong. Delpha had reclaimed her spot next to King Stern and was busily repeating everything she had already informed him of earlier. Only this time, Delpha emphasized just how bizarre she thought Clara had been acting, and all the while, mocking her about losing her lyre, and especially for living with people!

Carried away with trying to make Clara look foolish, Delpha cut a swatch of netting from the edge of the table covering and quickly placed it over her head. "And that strange garment she insists on wearing!" She grabbed a handful of sea fronds from a platter and dramatically stuffed them through the holes in the net to mimic Clara's garb, while she babbled on and on. "Can you believe how ***helpless*** she is? I certainly hope she finds her tribe." With that comment, Delpha realized King Stern's facial features had hardened, and immediately tried to smooth over her comments. "Once the cut on her forehead is healed, of course. We can't possibly let her leave before then."

"It's possible she may never be able to leave," the king declared.

"What?" Delpha blurted. "I'm sure she has her own tribe out there *somewhere!"* Delpha could no longer hide her defensiveness or her annoyance with the interest the king showed for Clara.

Stern retorted, "She has a terrible wound on her forehead, and she thinks she lives with *people*. That's why, Delpha! She's obviously in distress! And you just said it yourself—*she is helpless!* Do you really think we can just turn her away before she has recovered? And by the way, I *like* her garment."

The other sea maidens around the table were already busily cutting netting and decorating it, as they too, thought Clara's unique garment was actually quite beautiful.

CHAPTER THREE:

Calamities Exposed

In the wee hours of the morning, Thurlow woke to the sound of a thud hitting the floor. He crept out of bed and peeked into Alistur's bedroom. Surprisingly, Alistur was not in his room. He continued through the kitchen and the living area, making his way to the laboratory in the back of the house. There he discovered a dim lantern flickering. Looking closer, Alistur was fast asleep, slumped over a heap of books and scrolls strewn about the table. Standing over him, Thurlow's surprise was overshadowed with curiosity as to why his son had fallen asleep in the laboratory.

Gently nudging Alistur's shoulder, Thurlow lunged just in time to catch another book slipping from the pile. He carefully lifted Alistur's arm and draped it around his own shoulders. When he pulled his son away from the table, Thurlow caught glimpse of what Alistur must have been reading when he fell asleep. It was a small compendium written in Balthazar's own handwriting—a collection of methods for reversing spells. *Reversing spells? Why would Alistur be reading this, when he has the Shield?* he wondered.

Being only a few inches taller than his lanky son, Thurlow easily guided him away from the table. Standing him upright, he noticed the unsightly red marks on Alistur's face and ears. *The poor boy must have run head-on into a beehive,* he thought. As painful as the welts looked, he was surprised Alistur hadn't asked him to treat them. *Perhaps this is what he was trying to remedy when he fell asleep reading,* he thought.

Alistur trudged alongside without fully waking. When Thurlow lowered him onto the bed, Alistur only groaned and rolled over toward the wall.

Dawn was barely breaking, but Thurlow had no desire to go back to sleep—his mind was already churning. Having a full schedule of meetings with the king and other important advisors, he wanted to get the books put away and prepare a medicine for Alistur's welts before leaving for the day.

While Alistur slept, Thurlow returned to the laboratory. Perusing through the assortment of books, he was intrigued by the array of materials his son had gathered. Thurlow figured he must have been up most of the night poring over the vast collection of information piled on the table.

Knowing that Alistur had experienced repeated difficulty with the task of identifying herbs and various fungi needed for potions, Thurlow thought perhaps his son was just feeling anxious and wanted to review some things he was still unsure about. Or, maybe he had touched a poisonous plant while picking specimens—another likely cause for the welts on his face. After all, Alistur had failed the last plant-gathering task, and Thurlow had been a bit hard on him when explaining the consequences for selecting the wrong plants. It had happened during a recent exercise when he'd sent Alistur deep into the woods to gather exotic specimens. Instead of picking sweet Tesso leaves used for brewing tea, Alistur had picked leaves from a deadly Yagg plant by mistake. Thurlow had taken Alistur back to the same area in the woods to educate him about the slight—but extremely important, and sometimes fatal—differences of the characteristics between plant varieties such as the Tesso and Yagg plants. Thurlow had further explained how serious it could be if the wrong ingredients were used while making mild-altering concoctions such as sleeping potions or anecdotes for poisonous snake bites, among numerous other things.

The more he thought about Balthazar's handbook being on top of the pile, he became more than curious. It was hard to tell whether Alistur had merely been studying in general—in preparation for obtaining his crystal wand—or whether he was searching for something specific. The latter is what concerned him the most.

When Thurlow reached down to retrieve the fallen books, something else caught his eye. He stared for a long moment, hoping that it wasn't what it looked like. Frowning, he knelt down to examine the crevice around the door.

By design, it would appear that the wall was solid. But in reality, a section of the wall was actually a door—a concealed door used to access the Rabbit Hole. A small brick had been dislodged from its place and was lying on the floor in a small pile of crumbled mortar. Thurlow was almost certain the door to the passage had been compromised, believing someone had entered the laboratory from the tunnel. He carefully placed the brick back in its place and swept up the broken mortar.

Forgetting about the disarray of books for the time being, Thurlow scanned the bookshelves and scrolls tucked into small compartments in the wall, looking for signs of tampering. The most important thing he intended to investigate was the well-being of the Grimaldi Recordings.

Even though Thurlow had informed Alistur of the existence of the Recordings, he'd not yet enlightened him as to how to reveal and translate the writings held within the sacred binder, so he couldn't imagine his son would have attempted to remove the tome from its place.

The volume chronicles ancient family secrets passed down from Thurlow's ancestry, and illustrates diagrams and recipes for a substantial collection of potions, serums, spells, and medicines. However, even if an intruder could manage to get his hands on the antiquity, they would not know what to make of its peculiar contents without the use of an Obsidian Orb; a small, black pellet made from a blend of minerals, along with the most powerful of the crystal powders—the rare ebony.

Undeniably, his ancestors had gone to great lengths to protect their family secrets. Since Thurlow's grandfather, Balthazar, as well as his father, Florian, had passed on, Thurlow was now the only wizard left with the knowledge of how to reveal the encryptions and translate the language the Grimaldi Recordings had been written in.

Even the formula, and the alchemy process for making the mysterious Obsidian Orbs from ebony crystal powder was sacred. With himself being the only wizard with this knowledge, Thurlow was feeling the pressure to teach Alistur how to access and translate the Recordings, and how to concoct the necessary Orbs.

Even though he'd felt pressed to educate Alistur about the Recordings, he wanted to make sure Alistur was fully prepared to assume the responsibility. Thurlow had been holding off until after his son had harvested his crystal wand, and was keen to the intrinsic powers within crystal. Used carelessly, the temperamental ebony crystal had been known to wreak extreme havoc, eliciting great difficulty to control.

Stooping to the floor, Thurlow crawled beneath the table to remove a heavy stone from the supporting base. At that moment, while in the awkward position, he was grateful for his slim and flexible physique. Reaching his hand into the hollow of the base, he removed a thin slab of stone which was being used to conceal the floor opening. Propping the cover out of the way, Thurlow reached into the hole with both hands to retrieve a chest nestled below the surface of the floor. Working quietly, he placed the chest upon the table. He then crawled over to the opposing base and removed another specific stone in the floor. From inside that hollow Thurlow reached into its cavity, from which he pulled a large leather-bound book. The thick book was encased between iron hinges with clasps on all four sides. Each clasp folded to the center, tightly secured by an ancient locking mechanism—making it impossible to remove the pages without unlocking the clasps properly. From a tiny pocket inside his cloak, he pulled out a uniquely shaped key. Using that key, he unlocked the ornate chest first, from which he obtained a second key, using it to unlock the iron clasps securing the binder. He then opened the delicate pages to the marker placed in the precise center of the book. Opposing page numbers 276 and 277 *would* have appeared—if the pages were not totally ***blank***. He then removed an Obsidian Orb from the chest. Gripping the glittering, black pellet between his thumb and index finger, he burst the Orb and watched the smoky powder settle over the blank pages.

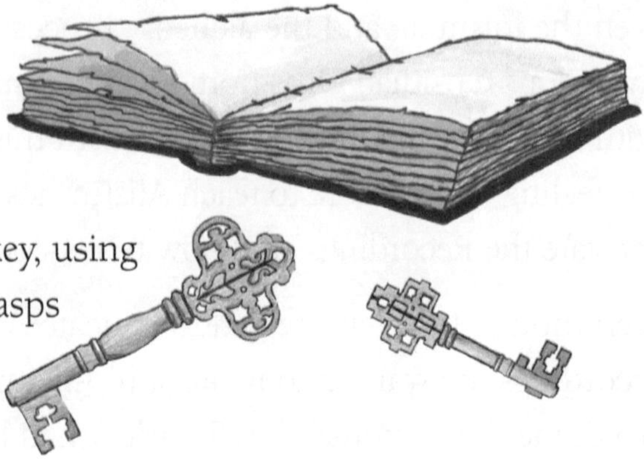

"Ahhh, perfect," he muttered. Gently fanning the pages with his hand, the fine powder gradually disintegrated, absorbing into the layers and layers of parchment. The familiar haze settled ever so gently, slowly revealing the encryptions. He carefully perused through the fragile pages, checking to see that everything was intact. Satisfied the Recordings had not been violated, he made a mental note to prepare a few more Obsidian Orbs for his cache. He patiently waited a few more minutes while the pages turned blank again and the effects of the powder wore off. Once the words disappeared, he locked the clasps back together and tucked the book back into its secret vault, then returned the chest to its place.

Curious if perhaps other supplies or concoctions had been disturbed, Thurlow turned his attention upward to the cabinet marked "Medicine." Other than the peculiar placement—high on the wall—the cabinet appeared to be a normal storage cupboard for medicines. When he opened the door, the first few things in sight were herbs, dried fungi, bandages, and other medicinal necessities. However, when the typical items were moved away, various apothecaries of colorful substances were revealed. The placement of the cabinet was necessary when Alistur was small because he was drawn to the jars containing the colorful crystal shards—*Sparkly Sands*—as Alistur had named the substances that could easily wreak tragedy in the hands of a young apprentice.

Thankfully, everything appeared to be untouched, leaving Thurlow dumbfounded as to the potential intrusion—and who the trespasser might have been.

With everything seemingly in order, Thurlow wondered if perhaps a hungry rodent had caused the small brick to dislodge. Hoping not to find a brood of rats eager to get inside, he decided to take a look through the tunnel for his own peace of mind.

After tiptoeing through the living space, and through the kitchen, he made his way to Alistur's bedroom to check on him. Finding his son soundly asleep, Thurlow went back into the laboratory and lit a torch. Entering the passage, he expected to face clusters of spider webs, but was quite surprised to find the space relatively clear, other than the scurry of a mouse or two. What he was not expecting though, was to see another torch propped near the doorway—smelling as though it had been used recently.

Walking through the tunnel, nothing else seemed out of the ordinary. Still concerned about the torch though, he continued looking. Within a couple of minutes, he'd made his way to the end of the passage without finding another clue as to what could have happened. Leaning his torch against the wall, he wriggled through the series of tight corners and stepped out into the entanglement of dried vines at the base of the steps. The sun was just beginning to rise in the royal gardens and the birds were chirping their morning calls. With just a quick glance around, he didn't see anything suspicious. Wishing he could stay and take in the beauty of the sunrise over the gardens, he could not afford the luxury this morning. Thurlow reluctantly reentered the dark passage, wanting to get back before Alistur stirred.

From what he could tell, there were no signs that the hidden entrance from the royal gardens had been exposed. The mysterious torch left near the door to the laboratory seemed to be the only alarming find. Thurlow second-guessed himself and wondered if he was simply becoming absent-minded. *Perhaps I left it there the last time I used the tunnel,* he thought. While staring at the ground, scratching the back of his head, a glimmer of light reflected off his torch to an object lying in the dirt.

It was Alistur's Shield! And it was supposed to be worn around his neck at all times, unless he was sleeping. *Lying there on the ground, with a broken cord, it was all but useless,* he thought.

Thurlow found it hard to believe that Alistur would defy the strict rules about the use of the Rabbit Hole without an extremely good reason. *And secondly, the Shield should never be out of his reach. Why would it be in the Rabbit Hole, and how did it get there?* he pondered. Thurlow tucked the Shield inside his cloak, and tried to come up with possible explanations.

When he re-entered the laboratory, he brought both torches inside and finished putting the books and scrolls away. Then he went to the kitchen to make breakfast and waited for Alistur to wake.

CHAPTER FOUR:

Fire-Breathing Beasts

Alistur woke to the pain of stiff and aching muscles, but wasn't clear-headed enough to recall the source of his ailments— or even remember putting himself in bed. Still tired, but too sore to lie there any longer, he slowly rose and stretched, trying to recall his actions of the night before. Drawn to the aroma of fresh-baked bread, he shuffled into the kitchen. With his grogginess slow to wear off, he had no idea just how disheveled he looked.

His face felt hot and tight around the welts and his eyes were bloodshot from lack of sleep. His curly hair stuck out every which way from hours of running his fingers through it while scouring through the volumes of information in the laboratory. Taking his seat at the table, his father served him some warm bread and breakfast porridge.

"Good morning, Son. How did you sleep?" Thurlow eyed him curiously.

Not aware he was still wearing his tattered cloak, Alistur answered with a mouth full of bread, and without *truly* answering how he'd slept. "Very well. And you must have risen with the birds this morning, Father."

"And you must have been quite exhausted to fall asleep in your cloak." Again, Thurlow watched his son's face.

The bread lodged in his throat while Alistur struggled to swallow. And think. "It was a little chilly last night, and I must have fallen asleep without changing."

His father didn't reply and Alistur hoped that would be the end of the questions.

Thurlow waited until Alistur had finished eating breakfast to inquire about the marks on his face. "Did you have a losing battle with a swarm of bees, Son?"

"Uh, yes," Alistur lied, as he reached up to touch his face. "Yes, I did. But I think the stings are doing much better now and should be gone soon." Actually, he knew the welts weren't doing any better at all. In fact, they felt worse, and he flinched when he touched them. "They still hurt a bit when I touch them though."

"Those marks don't look as if they will be going away anytime soon." Thurlow spoke in a quiet tone, slowly massaging the stubble on his chin. "In fact, they don't look like any bee stings I've ever seen. They look worse than that, Son. *Much worse.* Was it a swarm of *ordinary* bees, or a hornets' nest, I wonder?" While noticing the battered condition of Alistur's cloak, the tone in his voice intensified. "And why is your cloak torn to shreds—*and singed?!*" Thurlow was ready to hear some answers.

Alistur quickly sat up tall and straight in his chair, staring into his empty bowl, as if he were recalling the scene, when in fact, he simply wanted to avoid meeting his father's eyes while trying to think of an excuse for the burns on his cloak. "I'm really not sure. I was up high in a tree when they swarmed me. I couldn't get down fast enough and I scraped my shins when I fell to the ground! See?" Alistur pulled up his cloak and pant legs to reveal the scrapes and bruises on his shins. Feeling a trickle of perspiration slide from the pit of his arms, he immediately felt ashamed for the lie he'd just told, and for avoiding the question about the burn holes.

"Since we don't know exactly what type of stings you have suffered, I believe we should call Horace Rhueder to see what he thinks. I'm sure he will know how to treat the blisters."

All color drained from his face except for the redness of the welts, and Alistur stiffened at the mention of the physician, knowing full well he couldn't fool the healer—a fact that would cause him even more shame once his father learned the truth. "Blisters?" His trembling voice escalated to a high pitch. "I have *blisters* on my face? We have nothing for these in our own medical supplies?"

"Son, if I don't know what caused the wounds, I cannot treat them effectively. You know what can happen when we speculate—I'm liable to treat you with something that could even make them worse. The healer has probably seen this type of sting before, and he'll know exactly what to do. I'll send for him as soon as I get over to the castle this morning."

Realizing this was his chance to come clean and accept his father's help, Alistur filled his cheeks with air and exhaled slowly before he finally spoke, thinking about how much worse the sores might feel after having them poked and prodded. "It's more than likely that *you* will know what to do about them. I don't think the physician will know how to handle these."

"Why is that? I'm not a physician," Thurlow stated.

"Because these aren't exactly *bee* stings."

"What then, are they? Exactly?"

"They are much worse than bee stings. They're dragonfly stings."

"*Dragonfly stings?* But dragonflies don't sting, Son. And they rarely bite unless threatened or provoked to do so."

"Well, these weren't *ordinary* dragonflies."

"What are you trying to tell me?" Thurlow's face left little doubt that he was getting short of patience.

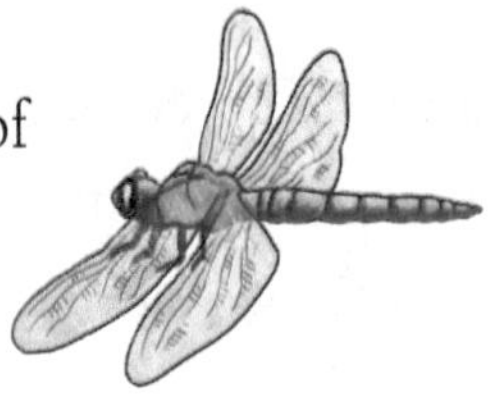

"I was practicing in the gardens, and a swarm of regular dragonflies flew through the spell and the next thing I knew I was being attacked by tiny, fire-breathing beasts! They spewed flames all around my head! And nearly caught my cloak on fire!"

Thurlow looked amazed, trying to visualize the scene. "That's a first! I don't believe I've ever seen such tiny flying dragons," Thurlow stated. "But now that I know those are *burns*, and not stings, I certainly know better how to treat them. Is there anything else I should know?"

With more angst than he'd intended, Alistur lashed out. "Like what? I was nearly scorched to death! Isn't that enough?"

"I just want to know how to help you, that's all," Thurlow asserted.

Feeling ashamed for his outburst and exaggeration, Alistur decided this was the time to tell his father the rest. After all, he needed his father's help—and the sooner, the better.

"Well, I'm sure the dragonflies are long gone, but there's some other birds and things that got in my way too. I've not been able to get them fixed yet. But I've tried, I *really* have."

"Other birds—and *things?* In the royal gardens? You know, if the mishap was a sincere mistake, your Shield should have helped you. Were you using it?" Thurlow looked him directly in the eye, while waiting for an answer.

Alistur lowered his eyes to the floor. "I forgot to take it with me. I came back to get it—but then it didn't work. I tried everything I knew, but the more I tried, things got worse and worse." A vision of Clara's face submerged in the stream with bubbles trailing from her nose formed in his mind's eye. He was consumed with guilt and anxiety—not knowing what had happened to her, or whether he could successfully get her back safely. With his stomach churning, he took a deep breath and readied himself to confess.

When he looked up, his train of thought faltered. His Shield was dangling from his father's fingers. Alistur's eyes bulged when he saw it, fearful of where his father might have discovered it. "Where did you find it? I was afraid it was gone for good."

“Where do you think I may have found it?” Thurlow pressed.

Alistur looked at the floor again as perspiration formed on his upper lip. “In the Rabbit Hole?” he asked sheepishly, trying with all his might to keep his breakfast down.

“Yes. I found it in the Rabbit Hole. You know the rules about using the passage, Son. Why were you in the tunnel? Were you in danger?”

“I wasn’t exactly in danger. The first time, I needed a short-cut to make sure no one saw me while I ran back home.”

“The *first* time?”

“After you were asleep last night, I used it again,” Alistur answered quietly. “I know it was wrong, but I was desperate to fix things without having to bother you.”

“So, these things that are not yet fixed—is that perhaps what you were studying last night?”

“Yes, I was trying to find some information that could help me.”

“Did you find the answers you were looking for?”

“No. I still need your help.” Alistur paused, hating more than anything to ask his father to rectify his blunders. But he had no choice. It was clearly time to ask for his father’s help. “Will you help me, Father?” His shoulders sagged in defeat. “Please?”

Thurlow took a deep breath before answering. “There will be a lot of activity around the castle compound later this morning, so we’d better go now. And as soon as we get back, I’ll mix up some ointment for those burns.”

Neglecting to clear the table, they hurried into the laboratory. Guilt washed over him again when Alistur saw two torches leaning in the corner near the door to the Rabbit Hole—proof his father had discovered the one he'd used the night before. Thurlow lit one and handed it to Alistur. "After you."

When they emerged through the other end of the passage, Alistur pointed toward the pond. "We need to go over there."

Looking out over the pond, it didn't take long for Thurlow to see what needed fixing. As the vibrant *swans* swam closer, he was appalled. "I assume there are peacocks needing my attention as well?"

"Yes, sir. They're right over there," Alistur pointed to the lackluster *peacocks*—minus their elegant plumage. The birds didn't seem to know any better, but Alistur was embarrassed enough for all of them.

"What else? What else do I need to see before we get started?" Thurlow inquired.

"We need to locate the flamingos…and a zebra," Alistur answered with remorse.

"A *zebra!?*" Thurlow looked around anxiously.

"Yes. Unfortunately, the zebra got in my way too." Once again, he felt discomfort rising from his stomach up through his chest. With a burning lump swelling in his throat, he closed his eyes and braced himself to tell the worst of it. "And Miss Cla—" Thurlow cut him off before her name left his tongue.

"In *your* way? Alistur, this is *their* habitat! *What were you thinking?* You're going to make me very old before my time, Son." Thurlow was angry now. "Insects are one thing, but I'm very disappointed that you interfered with these innocent creatures roaming the gardens."

Trying to avoid further lecture from his father and desperately wanting to redirect the focus from himself, Alistur skipped over telling about Miss Clara in that moment, and instead, decided to bring up things his Great-grandfather Balthazar had shared with him.

"Many times, Great-grandfather Balthazar said there was a story behind every deep crease in Grandfather Florian's face. Were they stories such as this?"

"No! I can assure you I've had my share of mistakes over the years, but nothing such as this. And I'm not in the mood to reminisce about my own blunders." Thurlow turned full circle, scanning the grounds for evidence of the mishaps.

Alistur quickly dropped the conversation and walked toward the edge of the stream, looking for the flamingos. He spotted the zebra first. It couldn't be missed, considering the ruddy pink color of its hide, and the fact it stood on only three legs, with one tucked up beneath its body while drinking.

"*What...?*" The corners of Thurlow's mouth threatened to form a hesitant grin.

"I still need to find the flamingos," Alistur muttered.

"I'm guessing they shouldn't be too hard to identify."

Within moments, the black and white striped flamingos meandered nearby.

"Interesting." Thurlow looked around. "Anything else to locate before I lose sight of these poor creatures?"

"No. Not really. Well, maybe just some fish and stuff in the stream." Alistur felt horrible about lying, yet again, especially now that his father was here to help him out of the mess. But with fingers crossed behind his back, he told himself it was *mostly* true. He was still worried sick about Miss Clara and Olivia's cat, but he couldn't bear to reveal that just yet, in hopes they would both return after his father performed the corrections.

"Fish?" Thurlow asked.

Alistur guarded the tip of his tongue with his teeth and kept quiet. He couldn't bring himself to elaborate about what had happened at the stream just yet.

Thurlow continued looking around, and thought long and hard before speaking again. "We are very short on time, so it's going to take both of us. While I stay here to keep watch over these poor beasts, I need you to gather a few things."

"Yes, sir," Alistur stated. "Tell me what you need me to do." Relief washed over him to know his father was now in control, and he was more than willing to do whatever his father asked of him.

"Go back to the laboratory and gather items from the medicine cabinet. Behind the herbs, where the apothecaries are filled with the varieties of crystal shards…you know, the Sparkly Sands."

Thurlow looked about, pondering his list of things he would need.

Of course! The Sparkly Sands will fix everything! Alistur thought. He could hardly wait to see how his father would use the powders, so he could then do the same to bring Miss Clara and Marigold back.

"I will need exactly one level scoop of the white, the blue, the grey, the pink, and the green—the *sage* green, not the bright green. Only use the specific measuring scoop inside each jar, and be extra cautious to place each color into its very own pouch. Do not get any of the colors mixed together." Thurlow was quick and precise with his instructions. "Do you understand?"

"I understand." With the zebra and the swans in mind, Alistur thought perhaps his father forgot to ask for a scoop of black. "What about the black?"

"The *ebony?* Absolutely not! We need only the five colors." Thurlow turned his back and muttered a comment under his breath, "We should hope that you never need the ebony to fix a blunder."

Thurlow waited until his son was well inside the passage on the errand, and then he wasted no time. He was confident he could reverse Alistur's errant spells without the use of the crystal powders, but he wanted Alistur to be gone long enough to give him enough time to do it. If perhaps, the reversals proved to be problematic, he would then have the help of the powders if necessary.

As it turned out, the corrections were not difficult for Thurlow. Regardless, this was not the kind of wizardry in which he wanted his son dabbling in. Alistur's acts had been reckless, and could easily have caused serious harm to innocent creatures.

Once he was satisfied that the mishaps were rectified, Thurlow remembered that his son had mentioned the fish. Peering into the stream, everything seemed normal. Without knowing precisely how the fish may have been affected, he quickly cast a spell for good measure, just in case any might be flailing about in distress. With a final look around, he quickly made his way toward the Rabbit Hole.

Back at the stream, out of Thurlow's line of sight, a catfish flipped high into the air, abruptly interrupting the zebra from drinking. It was not an ordinary catfish; it was *the cat*fish Marigold—the elusive creature Alistur would have given anything to capture.

Thurlow had to feel his way through the passage in the dark. More than halfway through, he saw light coming toward him. Before he could be seen, he called out, "Good news, Son! We're all done!"

Startled, Alistur stumbled and fell backward, dropping the torch. "You scared me! And what do you mean, *we're all done?* I needed to watch and see how you corrected my mistakes!" he shrieked.

"There's plenty of time to learn how to unravel mistaken spells, Son. For now, I'd like you to focus on not being careless."

Thurlow retrieved the torch and helped his son get to his feet. "Besides, there's some stirrings around the castle. Luckily, I was able to make the corrections without needing the crystal powders, and get out of the area before being seen."

Alistur was discouraged that he didn't get to watch his father. He was hoping to get an idea as to how he might conjure Miss Clara and Marigold back from the stream. On top of his sulky mood, he was gravely concerned about Miss Clara. His guilt was building up and he was feeling desperate.

Once they were inside the laboratory, Thurlow climbed onto the stepstool and asked Alistur for the powders. "Hand me the pouches, Son. I'll put the powders back and then mix up a remedy for those burns." Alistur handed him the four pouches from his right pocket. Underneath his cloak, he put his left hand in his other pocket and felt around for the fifth—shoving it deeper into his pant pocket. Alistur walked away from the cupboard, hoping his father already had his mind on the medicine he was preparing to make, without realizing he'd only handed him four pouches.

To the contrary, Thurlow immediately realized his son only handed him four pouches. He'd given him one simple task: collect five specimens. Just as he opened his mouth to scold him, he decided to let it go, blaming it on Alistur's sleep deprivation and what he was already dealing with.

Assuming Alistur had absent-mindedly forgotten to gather all five colors, Thurlow didn't mention the fifth pouch. His son was already disappointed that he didn't get to watch the corrections, so Thurlow let him off the hook for not gathering all of the supplies he had requested. Thurlow emptied the four pouches, and pushed the apothecaries to the back wall of the cabinet, then proceeded to collect the items needed to make the ointment, naming off the herbs he would use in the medicine. When he stepped down from the cupboard, his tone turned serious.

"That was the last time we will use the Rabbit Hole for frivolous reasons. As you very well know, the passage is to be used to protect the royal family. We can't afford having anyone realize its existence." Thurlow was very direct with his statements and didn't invite further conversation about it. "We are wizards, Alistur—*not street magicians*. We do not go around performing tricks for the entertainment and amusement of others, even ourselves. We possess extraordinary powers and along with that, comes responsibility. You have an obligation to respect your gift. If you wield your powers with wisdom and respect, you will not find yourself in these predicaments."

Alistur nodded his acknowledgment of the finality of his father's remarks.

Thurlow then turned his attention to making medicine, crushing a variety of dried herbs and fungi with a pestle. Adding another scoop of mugwort and a drizzle of olive oil, he mixed the ingredients into a thick paste and covered each blister on Alistur's head with a glob of the sticky, green concoction.

"I need to get over to the castle. We're finalizing rules for the Games, so I'll be away for several hours. I want you to stay indoors all day today and give these wounds a chance to heal, then I'll reapply more ointment when I return this evening. Do you understand?"

"Yes, sir." Alistur understood completely, and he hoped this would be the last time his father would mention the mishaps in the gardens. He wouldn't dare to venture outside with disgusting blisters and globs of goo all over his face. If having to stay inside was to be his only punishment, he was thankful. Besides, it would give him plenty of time to think about how he would use the sage green Sparkly Sand he had pilfered. He assumed anyway, that was the appropriate color to be used in the stream to conjure Miss Clara's return and reverse the spell to return Marigold to her former cat glory.

CHAPTER FIVE:

Conditions of the Agreement

By early afternoon, Princess Olivia had spent hours scouring the compound in search of Marigold, after the cat had failed to show up for breakfast. "Marigold! Marigold, *where are you?*" Undeterred by the hoarseness of her sore throat, she continued. "*Marrigoolld!*" Typically, Marigold spent her days bird-watching in the vast gardens, but she'd always been eagerly waiting to receive breakfast before skittering off in the mornings. "Don't worry, Marigold," Olivia's lips quivered as the words caught in her throat. "I'll keep looking until I find you!"

Taking a respite from her search, Olivia sat on the ground gazing out toward the coastal waters, hugging her knees to her chest. It was a clear and sunny day, although from her ground-level position, she couldn't see much beyond the LaMer Lighthouses. The identical twin beacons usually served as the prominent landmarks in her drawings. With one situated along the north-eastern coast of the Isle of LaMer, and the other along the rocky shore of Fleurbania, the imposing structures stand diligent in their perpetual duty, guiding vessels through the narrow waterways. Ornately crafted and easily identifiable as royal Fleurbanian landmarks, she'd sketched them hundreds of times.

The princess was aware of a beautiful lagoon further north called Goldfin Cove. The lagoon surrounded the ruins of her Great-grandmother Queen Ruthelda's cliffside summer palace, and was home to Aquan's Lighthouse—an incredible structure she'd only heard about, but never seen. The lagoon was rumored to be populated with merfolk and it was her aim to get a close look at the sea maidens someday—and of course, to sketch the extraordinary lighthouse in the cove.

Olivia never grew tired of fantasizing about the creatures of the sea and relishing in the lore of merfolk. Ancient tales of the realm suggest that a fabled mer-couple, King Aquan, and his beautiful queen, Myrth, had frequently occupied the top of the lighthouse in Goldfin Cove—using their intrinsic powers to keep the waters calm while guiding Fleurbanian vessels to safe harbor along the rugged coastline.

Forty years ago, during Queen Ruthelda's reign, a marvelous sculpture had been commissioned and permanently placed on a platform atop the lighthouse. Cast in copper, in enormous proportions, the subjects of the effigy are none other than the mighty King Aquan and Queen Myrth.

The mer-queen peers into the water with pursed lips, as though she's gently ushering a vessel along the coast, while King Aquan's muscled arm holds his trusty trident, thrust high into the sky, keeping a never-ending watch for dangers of the deep.

Of course, Olivia believed the fantastic tales were more than mere rumors and lore, because her mother had told her all about them and had promised to take her to Goldfin Cove to see the merfolk for herself one day. Sadly, it was a promise not kept. More than four years ago, when Olivia was only nine years old, her mother, Queen Giovanna, had mysteriously passed away while lying in her bed, cradling her newborn son. In a gut-wrenching twist of fate, the infant prince she had given birth to only one day earlier, died in her arms. Within mere seconds of the queen's last breath, the infant slipped into a peaceful sleep in his mother's loving embrace, and never woke. Even though the whispered rumors spoke of sabotage and poison, the cause of their deaths remains a heartbreaking mystery to this day.

~

Straining to see further north, Olivia craved for a better view. She raced across the gardens to the castle, and up the winding stairs to her father's private chambers. From the turret, the view was splendid—especially with the use of a special instrument Thurlow had given to her father. He'd crafted a thin, crystal disc to fit perfectly inside a long tube of embossed silver. Thurlow called it a spy scope. When held close to the eye, the scope clarified details of distant images and made them appear to be much closer. By using the scope, Olivia could see a vast length of the shoreline, until it curved. Much to her disappointment, Goldfin Cove, which she desperately wanted to see, was well beyond the curve. However, being at least a couple of hours by horseback over rough terrain, her father had forbidden her to travel that far up the coast alone. For now, she had no choice other than to rely on her imagination.

Peering through the scope, Olivia watched the waves breaking against the shore, and the hungry herons hovering above the sea foam. Slowly inching her line of sight up the coast, she gazed upon the skinny palm trees sprouting from the craggy shoreline. Curiously, the palms along the very edge of the shore had grown practically sideways, reaching out over the water. "Oh, this is a fantastic scene," she commented.

Olivia settled into her father's big, comfortable chair with her sketchpad propped in her lap. Inspired by a combination of the view of the pretty Isle of LaMer and her vivid imagination, she spent a couple of hours creating pages upon pages of different scenes along the coast—complete with dolphins and various fish species of her fancy. She skillfully added images of sea maidens frolicking about. Of course, she didn't actually see the merfolk with her own eyes, she merely drew images to her liking. Satisfied with her drawings for the day, Olivia packed up her work, and made another round through the castle grounds, scouting for any sign of Marigold.

Saddened by her futile efforts, Olivia went to bed a second night without Marigold curled up at her feet, and vowed another tearful promise to find her the next day.

ᔓᔕ

The next morning, Olivia woke thinking about Marigold. "This will be the day I find her," she declared. After quickly gathering the spy scope and her sketching supplies, she tried to skip breakfast so she could begin her search. Not hungry, all she really cared about was finding her cat.

Olivia tried in vain to skirt around the kitchen and head out the door. Just as she neared the kitchen though, her Aunt Mimi stood directly in her way with her hands parked on her hips. "Good morning, Princess," Mimi said cheerfully. "Put your things down and join us for breakfast."

Mimi's role within the royal family had shifted when her sister, Queen Giovanna, passed away. Although she was no longer needed as the queen's trusted confidante, she provided much-needed comfort to her three young nieces, and vowed to stay with them for as long as they wished her to remain.

Knowing she wouldn't get anywhere arguing with Mimi, Olivia reluctantly put down the burlap bag and took her seat at the long table. "Where's Lilian?" Olivia asked.

"Your sister has not come down yet. She should be along any time though," Mimi answered.

"She probably won't come down again this morning," Gabriella insisted with a mouth full of bread. "She's too nervous about the upcoming Games—and her *husband-to-be.*" Gabriella puckered her lips and made a smacking noise. "It's true," she continued, licking jam from the tips of her fingers. "She stays in her chamber all day, fretting."

"Gabriella! Shame on you! Lilian has every right to feel nervous," Mimi scolded.

Gabriella rolled her eyes. "I shall only marry for *love*. I would never allow the Games of Invasion to choose my betrothal."

"You won't have to! *You are not father's heir, because you are only sixteen!* Lilian is the heir, and father has decreed that she will marry the *best* knight in all the kingdom!" Olivia smugly interjected. "Then father will make him a prince!" she added matter-of-factly. "And besides, even though I'm the youngest, I too, shall want a worthy knight to be my husband when I marry."

"You're only thirteen! You are *years* away from marrying anyone at all!" Gabriella giggled at her sister. "And by the way, Lilian's husband shall become the prince *consort*—for having the privilege of marrying the heir to the throne. Anyway, Lilian already knows in her heart whom she wishes to marry," Gabriella mused.

Olivia scooted to the edge of her seat, eager to hear more of the gossip her older sister shared.

"I think she's known this for all of her life." Batting her lashes, Gabriella leaned forward and whispered the name. "Latticus of Persicoh."

"Latticus of Persicoh? Do you think he will win? Father says there will be more than one hundred knights competing. And that's why he says the Games are *extra* dangerous this year!" Olivia noted.

"This is true. And Lilian can hardly bear the thought that Latticus will have to fight against all of them to win her betrothal."

Deciding it was time to change the subject, Mimi placed a plate of pandemain bread and a small bowl of porridge in front of Olivia. "Where are you off to so early, Liv?"

"And what's in that bag you've been carrying around?" Gabriella asked before Olivia could answer Mimi.

"My sketchpad…" with hesitancy, she thought it best to also mention the other item in her bag, since she hadn't asked permission to borrow it. "And father's spy scope. I'm searching for Marigold." Olivia didn't want to tell them she also uses it for sightseeing while sketching, because she didn't want to take the time to share her recent drawings.

"Through the *spy scope?* Just how far do you think she's gone?" Gabriella chided.

"It's very helpful for looking all through the gardens," answering in between hurried spoons of porridge, "I can see much better with it."

"Don't worry, she'll come back when she gets good and hungry," Gabriella declared, with a dismissive wave of her hand.

Olivia took the last bite of bread with her and left the table. As she headed for the door, Mimi wrapped up a spiced crunchy biscuit. "Here, put this in your bag, Liv. I don't want you to get hungry while you're out looking for Marigold," Mimi smiled. "You will find her, don't worry." With a hug, Mimi gently kissed her forehead.

Olivia slung the bag over her shoulder, and headed toward the gardens, calling for Marigold. Eventually, she ended up in front of the main fountain where she unpacked her supplies, and spread her drawings on the steps around her. Stretching her long legs out in front of her, she expertly braided her long, honey-blonde hair into a thick braid down one side of her head, while surveying her work.

Distracted by footsteps, Olivia frowned when she saw Alistur coming her way. Slightly irritated at her best friend for not coming around the day before to help her look for Marigold, she quickly cast her eyes back to her sketches.

"Good morning," Alistur said, knowing full well she would not be in a good mood.

Olivia ignored him and continued sorting through her work.

He tried again, this time with a formal bow. "Good morning, Princess Olivia. May I ask what you are so busy with this morning?"

Without looking up, she answered. "I might ask you the same thing."

"What's wrong?" Feeling immediately guilty, he knew her dour attitude more than likely had to do with her missing cat. "Are you angry with me?"

"Considering you are supposedly my best friend, yes. I could have used your help yesterday, that's all. I've been looking everywhere for Marigold and I can't find her." Olivia's nose reddened and tears threatened to spill from the corners of her eyes.

"I'm sorry. I couldn't come out yesterday, Liv. Father required me to stay inside with healing medicines," he answered sheepishly.

Olivia tried to act uninterested, but when she looked up, his unsightly appearance caught her by surprise. "What happened to your face?" she blurted.

"A run-in with a swarm of bees," he fibbed, shifting his weight nervously from one foot to the other.

"Bees?" Her bright blue eyes filled with fear, as if the bees were still trailing him. "Around here?"

"No, not around here. You're safe." He gazed toward the stream as they talked. "What else did you do yesterday?" Unfortunately, Alistur noticed nothing unusual in the stream while making small talk.

"Besides looking for my cat, I sketched." She stared at his face, feeling slightly sorry for him.

Awkwardly, he tried to show interest in her sketches. "Were you busy sketching more of your fantastic sea creatures?" he grinned.

Olivia raised her brows at the remark, but gave him no reply. Usually, Alistur never showed much interest in her drawings, even though he regularly teased her about her wild imagination. She ignored him a little longer, hoping he would leave so she could get back to her work. He didn't.

"Actually, I sketched from my father's turret yesterday. I had a splendid view toward Goldfin Cove through the spy scope." She stretched the truth about being able to see anywhere near the cove, but she wanted him to think she'd seen it. The reality was, beyond the farthest point to which she could actually see, she had only sketched what she imagined the scenes *might* look like.

"*Goldfin Cove?* You can see all the way to the cove through the spy scope?" He stared down at the artwork spread out around her. "I've never been there! Can I see them?" Alistur's *hope* that she'd sketched Goldfin Cove was clouded by the fact that he should have realized she couldn't possibly see that far up the coast, even with the spy scope.

Olivia quickly decided to use Alistur's eagerness as leverage to her advantage. "On one condition," feigning more confidence than she actually felt.

"What's the condition?"

"After you look at my drawings, you will help me look for Marigold, and you will continue helping me until we find her."

Although his face was already red and puffy, it reddened deeper in response to Olivia's innocent request. Immediately, guilt washed over him, making the blood drain as quickly from his face as it had entered. "I promise. I'll help you look for her," he muttered.

Olivia tilted her head, with brows raised, waiting for him to qualify his remark.

"*Until we find her,*" Alistur conceded, reaching for the sketches.

"Sea maidens? You saw *merfolk?*" he asked, sorting through the illustrations with great enthusiasm.

"Well, not…" her voice trailed off. "Not…exactly."

Alistur wasn't listening anyway. He was staring at the images of merfolk frolicking among various other sea creatures of her making. Shuffling through the drawings, he was totally enthralled. "That's it! That's where she is! *Goldfin Cove*—of course!" he exclaimed, gazing in the direction toward the cove, totally unaware that he was thinking aloud.

"That's where *who* is?" Olivia stared at him, curiously. "Alistur? Answer me! What are you talking about?"

"Olivia, I truly believe we will find Marigold. Just give me your word that you will help me with something first. Please, Liv? It's important."

Curious as to his excitement about the sea maidens she'd drawn, and his impassioned interest in Goldfin Cove, she wanted to know more about his odd enthusiasm.

"You have my word. What exactly, do you need *my* help with?" Olivia wanted her cat back, so she was game for anything, but she fully intended to hold him accountable to the conditions of their agreement.

Alistur thought it might be a good idea to ask in advance for her leniency for what he was about to tell her. "Promise you won't get mad?"

He ignored the fact his question went unanswered. Alistur had no idea how he was going to explain everything to Olivia, but he'd already said too much. As witnessed, she had shown a rather unpleasant side of her personality and he sure didn't want to be on the bad side of a scorned princess, so he decided to give her the upper hand and let her know that he actually *needed* her help.

"Liv, I made a big mistake right here at the fountain a couple of days ago."

Olivia gazed around the fountain looking for evidence of what he may have done, then looked at him pointedly before opening her mouth to speak.

"Just let me finish what I need to say," he mumbled in a flustered tone. He paced a few steps, and started again. "I was practicing nearby, and…and one of my spells went terribly wrong. Miss Clara was here, singing. But, then she tripped and…and she fell into the stream." He turned his back on Olivia and started pacing again, with his hands clasped tightly behind his neck.

"So, did you help her out?" Olivia's question went unanswered, and her patience quickly grew thin.

"Alistur? Did you help Miss Clara out of the water?" she repeated.

"No," he answered meekly. "I couldn't."

"What do you mean, you *couldn't?* What happened to her?" Rimmed with confusion, her blue eyes turned icy and bore into his. "You said she was singing. So, how did she fall into the stream?"

"She tripped over her suitcase and fell into it." Alistur did not elaborate on the *reason* Clara tripped.

Peering into the water, Olivia suddenly spun around to face him. "You weren't able to save her? Are you trying to tell me that Miss Clara *drowned?* Why couldn't you save her, Alistur?" nose to nose she glared at him, in horror of what she thought he'd done. "Poor Gemma and Giles!" Olivia wailed. "They must be heartbroken." Olivia sobbed harder.

"I haven't spoken with Gemma and Giles yet, because…" his voice trailed off when Olivia reeled on him again.

"What do you mean you haven't spoken with them yet? You said this happened a couple of days ago, Alistur!" Olivia's face was beet red, overcome with both fury and sadness.

"I have time, Liv. Miss Clara won't be missed for a few days…she was on her way to Saint Richarde…"

Olivia shrieked. "*She won't be missed?* So that's why you haven't told anyone?"

Alistur shuddered when Olivia's eyes pierced into his again. Wringing his hands in frustration, he realized he was bumbling what needed to be said. "Because she's still alive! I know she is!" he blurted. "She looked right at me, Liv! I truly believe she is alive!"

"Then, where did she go?" Olivia looked at him with a blatant look of astonishment, which quickly turned to confusion. "You're scaring me, Alistur."

"The spell…" he faltered, and started again. "Liv, I know this is confusing, and you're angry with me right now. But…you are my very best friend, right?"

"I'm not so sure, Alistur! What does that have to do with any of this?" she shouted. "Poor Miss Clara! *What did you do?!*" She shook her head in anguish.

"Liv, please. You are the only one I can trust to help me. Please, just listen to me. I truly believe she is alive—but the spell turned her into a sea maiden, Liv. And it's all my fault!" As soon as he'd said it, he realized it was only what he *hoped* had happened, without realizing how ridiculous it sounded.

"Are you *crazy?* You turned Miss Clara into a sea maiden? You can't turn people into sea creatures, Alistur!" Olivia glared at him in disbelief. "Bring her back! Do you hear me? You've got to bring her back! You *can* do that, can't you?" Olivia marched up and down, peering into the stream.

"I'm trying to explain what happened, but I really don't *know* how it happened, because I didn't do it on purpose! I'm telling you that I believe Miss Clara turned into a sea maiden, and I'll bet she went to Goldfin Cove! She may very well be one of the sea maidens you drew in your sketches!"

Ironically, it was now Olivia's turn to confess. She stopped marching, and started to tell him that she hadn't drawn *actual* sea maidens. Even though Alistur was quite enthusiastic and hopeful about Miss Clara being one of the merfolk in her sketches, she needed to let him know the truth.

"Alistur, I didn't…" she was cut short again.

Alistur wasn't listening. He was babbling. "I can get her back! I have what I need to get her back!" He pulled the pouch out of his pocket. "See?"

"What's that?" Olivia frowned.

"This is Spark—uh, this is crystal powder. It's very powerful, and it will bring them back. You'll see." Alistur slapped his hand over his mouth. Again, he'd said too much.

"*Them?* Who else fell into the stream, Alistur?" Olivia demanded an answer.

Having no choice, he admitted the rest. "She accidentally pulled Marigold into the water with her, Liv." Then he clenched his jaw and waited for the outrage.

"*Marigold?!* Marigold fell into the stream with Miss Clara? *You let my cat drown?"* Olivia started sobbing and screaming all over again. "I hate you, Alistur!" Olivia shrieked through her sobs. "Why didn't you tell me all of this? I really and truly hate you!"

"Olivia, please listen to me. I believe Marigold is fine. She was actually swimming! I saw it with my own eyes—she didn't drown! She appeared to be…part fish and part cat, Liv. I watched her going along with the current!" He failed to mention she was squeaking hideously while sailing downstream.

Olivia could barely choke out the words. "You're telling me she was part *fish*—but yet, she is *fine?*"

"What I mean is…" Alistur struggled to explain what had happened. "It was because of the spell. That's why I know she will be fine. I'll reverse the spell, Liv. But I need you to help me. We're going to get Marigold back. And Miss Clara too."

As Alistur opened the pouch, Olivia glared at him with tears running down her face.

Alistur muttered a few words beneath his breath, then slowly poured the powder into the stream and waited. Nothing happened. Minutes passed, and still nothing.

Discouraged at the results, Olivia scolded him. "I really don't know what you expected to happen with that trickle of green sand you poured into the water, Alistur. It probably wasn't even enough."

"You don't know how these things work, Liv."

"*Apparently, you don't either!*" She turned her back and started gathering her things.

"Where are you going?"

She shot him a hateful look, that quickly turned to grief. "To be alone, Alistur! Without *you* anywhere near me!"

Wracked with guilt, he truly felt sorry for her—and ashamed of himself. "Wait! Please wait, Liv. I have more!"

"You have more *what*? More bad news?"

"I can get more of this. It's in my father's laboratory." He knew he wasn't supposed to invite anyone into the laboratory, but at this point, his poor judgement had placed him well beyond bending the rules.

"Oh! More green sand to pour in the water?"

"Please believe me—this is more than just sand. These are shavings from powerful crystals. It's what our wands are made of."

"Then I dread the day you receive a crystal wand, Alistur," Olivia scoffed.

"Please, Liv. Help me—and I promise we will get Marigold back." Alistur felt miserable and he was sorry he hadn't told his father about everything when he had the chance. If he'd done so, perhaps both Marigold and Miss Clara would be safe and sound. Olivia was truly his best friend—more accurately, his only friend—so it pained him to see her so hurt. At this point, he would gladly accept whatever punishment would come his way if he could take back the anguish he'd inflicted upon her.

In steely silence, Olivia trudged along beside him toward the Grimaldi quarters.

Before entering, Alistur looked around to make sure they were not seen entering together and made Olivia promise not to reveal that she had visited the laboratory. "I promise, Alistur! Who would I want to tell? Who would care anyway?" Alistur didn't answer as he held the door open for her and led her through their kitchen, and living area, to the rear of their quarters where the laboratory was located.

Olivia's eyes grew wide in fascination as she took in the chaotic ambiance of the laboratory. She could never have imagined the laboratory would look the way it did. It was much larger than she expected it to be, and one entire wall served as a small library. Shelves from floor to ceiling were bulging with books. Some were obviously ancient, with their tattered bindings barely holding together. Rows and rows of scrolls tied with colored strings and identification tags were tucked neatly in compartments. Hourglasses full of sand, vials, and vessels of all sizes were filled with various substances, covering most of the counter spaces. Bunches of dried herbs and flowers were labeled and strung on cords. Light-catching prisms hung from the cross-beams, sending radiant arcs of color racing through the air. Larger dried plants hung from the rafters. Windows placed high above in the ceiling allowed for plentiful light throughout. Upon closer inspection, even though the shelves, cupboards, and tables were covered with items, the chaos had a sense of organization.

"What we need is up there—in the medicine cabinet," Alistur pointed above her head.

"Medicine cabinet?" Olivia wrinkled up her nose at the thought and put her bag down.

"Never mind, I'll explain later. I'm going to climb up on the step stool and hand down what we need. Please be very careful when I hand you the jar, alright?"

Alistur stood on the tips of his toes, reaching around the medicinal supplies to get to the containers full of ground crystals. He moved the jars around to find the color he needed. "Are you ready?" He scooted the vessel to the edge and gripped it with both hands.

"Yes, you can hand it to me. I'm ready."

"Be very careful, Liv. It's kind of heavy. And make sure the lid stays on," Alistur cautioned. As she reached up, he handed the apothecary down to her. "Got it?"

"Yes, I've got it. Oh—it is heavy!" she groaned.

Alistur closed the cabinet door and stepped down. "Let's go. I'll carry it to the stream. I'm not sure how much we'll need, so I'll just take this and bring the rest back."

As they walked back through the gardens, Olivia quizzed him about the substance. "So, what *exactly* is this?"

"Basically, it's pure crystal that's been ground from solid forms. Like I mentioned, it's the same stuff our wands are made of, but it's even more powerful in this form. It's just what we need in order to bring Marigold and Miss Clara back." Alistur exuded more confidence than he actually felt in that moment. He mustered his confidence by reasoning that his father had more than likely intended to use the other four colors to reverse the spells on the animals in the gardens, so he believed the sage green powder was the color he needed to rectify the mishaps in the stream.

When they reached the stream, Alistur stood in silence for a long moment—analyzing the best way to conduct the spell. Setting the jar on the low barrier next to the water, he took off his shoes and rolled up his pant legs, exposing his skinned-up shins. Olivia frowned at the unsightly bruises and scrapes. "What…?" she shuddered, but didn't complete her question. "Never mind."

Glad she didn't ask for an explanation, Alistur took the lid off of the jar. "I need to get into the water, so don't let this spill." Actually, he didn't know if he truly needed to get into the water or not, but he thought it might be best. After he stepped over the barrier, Olivia carefully handed him the container.

Alistur placed the vessel in the crook of his arm and whispered undetectable words as he waded around. Moving ever so slowly, he tossed out a few handfuls of the powder. Suddenly, he winced in pain, and pitched the whole container up into the air! "Ouch!" he screamed, as the shards rained down around him.

"What happened?" Olivia shrieked.

"I stepped on something sharp!" Alistur limped around in agony and horror. "No, no, no!" he wailed. Trying to save any of the shards at all proved to be impossible. The tiny grains sifted right through his fingers and were quickly swallowed up by the current. Angrily, he scooped up the empty vessel before it sunk and handed it to Olivia.

Suddenly, the water began stirring and sloshing violently. "Olivia, look! It's working!" Alistur clapped his hands together as hordes of fish swam upstream against the current.

Within seconds, catfish were piling up all around him, and a few flopped over the edge. Olivia scrambled around, rescuing the fish on the ground and tossing them back into the stream. "It's *working?*" She looked disgusted again. "This is what you *wanted* to happen, Alistur?"

Hundreds of fish shot up into the air like a geyser. "These are *catfish,* Liv! Don't you see?" Trying to buy some time, Alistur tried to make her think it was all part of his grand plan. But the trouble was, they were just *ordinary* catfish. Where was the one he was trying to conjure? The one with the fluffy head of a cat—Marigold's head? Where was *that* one? *And where was Miss Clara?* he wondered.

Soon, the current calmed and changed directions. "No! Don't go! Not yet!" Alistur yelled as the fish receded downstream. There'd been no sign of either Marigold or Miss Clara.

Once the fish were gone, Alistur collapsed to the ground in defeat. Holding his head in his hands, he was exhausted. And soaked.

"Well? What now?" With her hands on her hips, Olivia glared at him through wet strands of hair stuck across her face.

"We have no other choice," Alistur quietly declared.

"What do you mean we have no other choice? I want my cat back, Alistur!" Olivia was furious. "And what about Miss Clara? You promised this would work!" she berated him.

"I mean, we have no other choice but to go to Goldfin Cove. That's where we'll find them."

“Goldfin Cove? We’re going to Goldfin Cove?” Olivia’s attitude slightly improved.

Alistur’s mood was still dour, and he was not as excited about the trek as Olivia seemed to be. He’d desperately hoped the crystal shards would have brought them back.

“There’s nothing else we can do today. I’ll meet you here tomorrow morning. I’ll be here early, so just come as soon as you’ve had breakfast and we’ll leave. I’ve never been there, so I don’t know exactly how long it will take. Probably a couple of hours—and possibly more.” Dejected, Alistur spoke without even looking up. “We can ride together on my horse.”

“Alright. I’ll see you in the morning, Alistur.” Olivia started for home. “I’ll ask Mimi to pack a picnic for us.”

CHAPTER SIX:

The Accidental Queen

Anxious about the day ahead, Alistur had been wide awake for quite some time, thinking about the trip to the cove, but stayed in his room until he heard the door close behind his father. Happy to find the kettle still hot and the bread his father had left for him still warm, Alistur gulped down a mug of tea and devoured a large chunk of the bread on his way to the stable.

Olivia was ready and waiting when Alistur arrived at their agreed upon location.

"Good morning, Liv. Are you ready?"

Olivia checked the contents of her bag one more time to make sure she had everything: waterskin, two wedges of flatbread, several pieces of dried meat, two sweet cakes, and of course her sketching supplies. "I'm ready," she confirmed, tucking the provisions into the saddlebag with Alistur's supplies.

Taking Alistur's hand, she hoisted herself up onto his horse, and situated herself behind him. Being at least an inch taller than Alistur, she could easily see the view ahead as they made their way toward a small field of wild snapdragons.

"Are you certain you won't be missed today by your sisters?"

"Not likely. Lilian has been secluded in her private chamber for days, and Gabriella is consumed with plotting her usual shenanigans. Just wait until you see what she has planned for the opening ceremony of the festival!"

"Oh? What's her plan?" Alistur asked.

"I'd like to tell you, but I'm sworn to secrecy. All I can say about it, is that you won't believe your eyes! Even for Gabby, this is the most outrageous thing she's ever schemed," Olivia giggled. "It's even *dangerous!*"

"Sounds intriguing!" Alistur commented. "And what about you? Will you be performing with the Cygnets again this year?"

"Oh, yes, in the group dances. It's not my favorite thing to do, but it makes my father happy to see us in the ballet. And Lilian has a solo performance this year—only one day after she finds out who her husband will be! I sure hope she feels like dancing," Olivia mused.

They rode alongside the stream, chatting, for half a mile before Alistur felt Olivia's hand slap at his back.

"Stop! Alistur, let me off! Stop!" She slid off before he could halt the horse.

"What is it?" Alistur turned the horse around to see Olivia scoop a scruffy, orange cat into her arms.

"Marigold! You came home!" Cooing in her ear, Olivia held her cat tightly, nuzzling it against her neck. "I knew you would come back to me." Marigold rubbed her head under Olivia's chin. "I can't believe it, Alistur! She's finally back!"

Alistur jumped down, very happy, and somewhat surprised to see that it was indeed Marigold. "See, Olivia? It worked! I told you it would work," he said, trying to convince himself as much as her, considering the fact he hadn't really known for certain how to reverse the devastating spell. "Marigold is fine—see?" Alistur eyed the cat, sincerely hoping all was well with the feline, but wondering why the crystal shards had not brought Miss Clara back as well.

Olivia didn't answer. Still cradling her cat, she sniffed back tears of joy. Purring in the nest of her limbs, Marigold, too, seemed quite happy to be back to normal.

Looking bedraggled though, the cat's fur was matted with shreds of sea leaves and she smelled horrendous. "*Where have you been?*" Olivia wrinkled her nose, but kept hugging the cat, regardless.

Alistur peered into the stream, hopeful for any signs of Miss Clara's presence. Nothing. After a couple more minutes, he suggested they get going.

"Are we ready, then? I'm certain she'll be waiting for you when we get back." No answer. "Are you sure you want to go with me, Liv? We don't have to stay very long. But, you don't have to go if you'd rather stay here with Marigold. I'll understand."

"She's probably hungry," Olivia cooed.

"Hungry? Look at her! That belly is fat with fish!" Alistur chuckled. "Looks like she's been eating her way through the stream."

"You're right. She's probably had plenty to eat." Olivia nuzzled Marigold for a long moment. "I've missed her so much, and I'd like to snuggle with her all day! But, she seems to be okay, and I've always wanted to go to Goldfin Cove…so, yes, I still want to go." Olivia kissed her cat one more time before turning her loose, smiling as Marigold ran off to chase after a bird. "Yes, she seems perfectly fine. I'm ready now."

∾

Alistur guided his horse around the outskirts of Ellinwood Hollow, toward the Westridge Trail. After traveling for almost an hour and a half, Olivia spotted steam rising from the ground in the distance. "Look, Alistur!"

"We're getting close!" Alistur concurred. "The vapors are from the hot springs." Focusing on the architectural ruins in the distance, Alistur plotted the rest of their journey.

"This is so exciting, Alistur! For as long as I can remember, I've wanted to trek this far up the coast, but father said there's really no need to travel here, with nothing but old ruins left since the Invasion."

"No doubt, he fails to understand your reasoning for wanting to come, considering your fascination with merfolk." Alistur smiled over his shoulder, glad Olivia's mood had lifted after finding Marigold.

"You're probably right about that," Olivia giggled. "Father said the numerous attacks by the Bruelanders caused Queen Ruthelda's palace to practically topple into the sea! I'm sure it's painful for him to see the remains of his grandmother's palace in such ravaged condition."

"My Great-grandfather Balthazar spoke many times of the conquests of the great warrior, Queen Ruthelda," Alistur noted.

"I've heard my father say we can all be thankful that the queen was not in residence during the Invasion, or he would never have been born," Olivia mused. "I wonder what would have happened if she'd been there at that time?"

"It's possible the kingdom would have fallen to the barbarians," Alistur answered. "I'm glad we'll never know."

They rode in silence for several minutes, before the lagoon edged into distant view.

"Let me see the spy scope, Liv." Alistur halted the horse to scan the landscape. "The ground is getting very steep and rocky. I don't think we're going to get close enough to see anything, because of the path we took. There's at least a half-mile of very rough territory between here and the lagoon side of the palace. All I can see is a small herd of wild goats and large rocks. Definitely not a suitable course for us."

Olivia groaned. "What can we do?"

Alistur handed the scope to Olivia. "Take a look slightly to the northwest. Do you see the lighthouse? That's the direction we need to go for access around the cove."

"Oh, I see it!" The copper figures at the top of the structure sent rays of sun bouncing high into the sky. "I can't believe I'm finally seeing Aquan's Lighthouse!" Even though she couldn't bring the shapes into clear focus, Olivia was thrilled, nonetheless.

After years of diligent duty, the sculpture had aged beautifully with a patina produced from oxidation, while panes of glass covering the windows sparkled with brilliant cataracts of salt from the sea.

"The sun is shining so brightly, I can barely make them out, but I know it's King Aquan and Queen Myrth!" Olivia squealed. "How can we get closer?"

"Remember that fork in the path, when the Westridge Trail ended? I believe we'll only need to backtrack for almost a mile, and then pick up the lower path, which will hopefully lead us to the coastal edge without being seen."

Olivia dug through the saddlebag for the sweet cakes. "Here, I brought these for us. Let's go."

Within thirty minutes, after traversing back down the steep, rough path they'd taken, they were finally on the right track, with the cove in viewing distance.

"Alistur, stop! Look—I think I see them!"

"I believe those are just dolphins, Liv. We'll need to get a bit closer to see directly into the lagoon."

Trekking higher up to a vantage point above the sea level, Olivia peered through the spy scope and let out a hushed squeal of delight.

"It's *them*—it's the merfolk without a doubt! They're swimming all about in the submerged parts of the palace! Take a look!" Olivia slid off the horse and handed Alistur the scope. "Listen! I can even hear their voices!"

Leaving the horse to graze, they crawled across the ground to get as close as they dared for a better look.

Alistur scanned across the water with the scope, hoping with every ounce of his being that he would lay eyes on Miss Clara. Searching for her brown hair, he quickly realized there were many sea maidens with various colors of hair. All of them had volumes of beautiful hair flowing about their bodies, but not even one had straggly, drab brown hair like Miss Clara's.

"Let me look again." Olivia eagerly reached for the scope. Intrigued by her first real look at the lovely creatures of the sea, she couldn't take her eyes away, slowly moving the scope about, taking in every inch of them. "They're all so beautiful!" Then she took notice of all the shiny adornments glinting in the sun. "And just look at the jewels they're wearing! Wonder where they got it all? Even the sea masters have gold around their necks!"

Tilting the scope, she noticed one couple secluded on a ledge jutting out from a glittering cliff, hovering just at the surface of the water. Bringing them into focus, she immediately noticed the wide band of decorative gold across the sea master's forehead.

"Take a look at those two nestled on the ledge. What is that across his forehead?" Handing the scope to Alistur, she quickly rummaged through her bag for the charcoal and began sketching.

"On the *ledge?* They can survive *out of the water?*" Alistur questioned.

"Of course, they can—for short periods of time," Olivia muttered. "They can actually do a lot of the same things we do." Olivia seemed to enjoy informing Alistur about the lore of the creatures of the sea. "You have a lot to learn about merfolk," she added.

"I see them. It appears he's wearing some type of emblem, and he's the only male wearing one. Perhaps it identifies his stature in the tribe." Then, he focused on the female. Volumes of chestnut colored hair cascaded down her back, but he couldn't see her face. "Let's try to move in a bit closer."

As they crept along they were careful to remain secluded in the tall grasses, while Alistur kept his eyes on the couple. "I think we can hear their voices better from here, echoing across the water," he whispered.

"And this is a much better angle for my sketching," Olivia whispered. "Now I can see their faces."

Taking turns looking through the scope, it seemed like Olivia took forever sketching the male's facial features. "What's taking so long? Try to get the sketches finished before they leave," Alistur whispered.

"I need to capture the details!" Olivia snapped.

"Shhh," Alistur put his finger to his lips. "If we can hear them, they can probably hear us."

Olivia was indeed taking her time. She worked on her subject's brows, the perfect slant of his nose, and his full lips. Slowly, his facial features materialized on her tablet. "The center piece on the band is definitely an emblem of some type, but obviously, I can't make out the details." When she was finally satisfied with the sketch of his face, she moved on to drawing his torso. With his flesh of golden-brown, he was a striking contrast to the fair-skinned sea maiden at his side. His wavy brown hair was generously sun-kissed with strands of buttery-gold, skimming just below his strong jawline.

Next, Olivia focused on the wide leather strap slung low across his waist—where his torso melded into its beautiful, scaled form, gleaming in iridescent hues of rich green and turquoise. Not able to make out the exact details, she reached for the scope again.

She could see it was an intricately tooled scabbard, with brilliant red gems sparkling from the handle of the dagger. She watched the sea master prop himself up on one elbow, as the two of them whispered back and forth, gazing into one another's eyes.

Once Olivia was satisfied with her rendering of the male, she turned her focus to his lovely companion. Compared to the other sea maidens, this one appeared to be even more exquisite. Her scaled form glimmered in hues of green and shades of deep lavender, and her tail fin was especially unique. Almost translucent, layers of shimmering iridescence flowed along her sides and from her tail fin. Even though all of them were wearing lots of jewelry, this maiden wore a special garment as well, decorated with small shells, and sea grasses.

"Wonder why she's all dressed up? She must be someone special," Olivia mentioned, as she diligently detailed the sizable, brilliant green gem hanging from a strand of very large pearls around the pretty maiden's neck. The pearls were unlike any she'd ever seen. Unique in their shape, they were exquisitely coordinated with the coloring of her lower body, reflecting rich hues of lavender and dark green.

When the sketches of the two were complete, she started on the breathtaking view surrounding the lagoon, trying to capture as many of the sea creatures as possible, and embellished the scene with the steam rising from the hot springs in the background.

Unable to hear most of the words the mer-couple spoke, they could detect only bits and pieces of the conversation. The maiden's tail fin gracefully raised and lowered, dipping into the water as she listened to the sea master's charismatic murmurs.

From the looks of it, the mer-couple were engaged in a meaningful and intimate discussion.

Alistur peeked his head above the grasses, straining to hear more of what the couple were saying. "Shhh." Alistur put his finger to his lips. "Stop sketching for a minute, maybe we can hear more."

Carried by a slight breeze, a few of the sea master's words echoed across the water: "…a lifetime…couldn't…lose you…belong with me…your people."

"No, no, no!" Alistur moaned. Then clapped his hand over his mouth, afraid they'd heard him. "Her *people?*" Alistur turned to Olivia and asked, "Did you hear that? I think he said she belongs with him—and something about her *people!* It's her, Liv—I know it's Miss Clara!" Alistur pounded his fist on the ground when he realized that Miss Clara might not be coming back to Mont Renault ever again. "Why would anyone believe this has happened?" he fretted. He brooded over the fact he'd procrastinated and had not told his father about Miss Clara. The situation was clearly out of control.

"We've got to get a bit closer, Liv. I need to hear exactly what they are talking about."

Olivia quietly put her supplies in the bag, and they slowly inched their way across the ground, finding little refuge, as the tall grasses and tumbleweeds became sparse.

They watched the sea master reach behind his back, into a netted bag. He pulled out an odd-looking item and presented it to his companion. Olivia grabbed the spy scope to get a closer inspection of what he gave to the maiden.

"What is it?" Alistur asked. "Olivia, what is it?"

When the sea maiden ran her fingers over the object, it became obvious.

"It seems to be a musical instrument. Listen—it sounds like a *lyre*," Olivia whispered, as they heard familiar chords the maiden plucked. "Hear it?"

The melody was a unique rendition of music Alistur had heard many times near the main fountain in the royal gardens.

"What is this wonderful instrument made of?" they heard the sea maiden ask.

Her companion proudly informed her of its making. "It's crafted from the skeleton of a large angelfish. I'm sorry you lost your lyre, so I hope this will do."

Holding it close to her body, the maiden giggled with delight.

"I'm glad it makes you so happy." Then he gently took her hand in his. "I wish to make you happy for the rest of your days."

Seemingly startled by his words, the maiden looked at him without uttering a word.

Gazing into her eyes, the sea master clarified his intent. "Clara, will you grant the honor of becoming my queen?"

"What? He just asked her to become his *queen!* Did you hear that, Olivia? He's the king of the tribe!" Alistur was panic-stricken. *"And he asked Miss Clara to become his queen!"*

"Well, by the looks of it, she has accepted!" Olivia exclaimed, as she watched the mer-couple embrace.

Alistur glared at them, his face ablaze as the remaining welts ignited in swollen color. "This can't be happening!" he whined.

The mer-king reached into the netted bag once more and pulled out a large seashell. The unique signal he blew through the conch summoned the entire tribe. The merfolk gathered at once, eager to hear what their king wished to say. His words rang out over the water, loud and clear: "Today, our tribe celebrates! Until now, I've been yearning for someone to capture my heart and soul—and to make our tribe whole! I believe Clara has answered that elusive desire and I feel as though I've been waiting a lifetime for her. She truly belongs with me, and with our tribe. I've asked her to become my queen, and I'm grateful to say, she has accepted!" Reaching into the bag one more time, the king pulled out a beautiful wreath of jewels and shells. He gently placed it atop her head, carefully weaving strands of her hair around the wreath to secure it firmly in place. "My Queen, you are one of us now, and this is your new beginning with our tribe. I would like to bestow a new name for you—if you so desire. It will become your Alecian name, and will symbolize permanence for our relationship. Please, choose any name you like, and it shall be yours. Take your time to think it over."

The tribe quietly watched and listened, eager to hear her response.

Clara put her hand across her heart, perhaps to make sure the pulses were real. She'd never experienced a happier moment in her entire life. When her fingertips brushed the emerald hanging from the pearls, she gently caressed the stone, and answered. "I do not need more time to think it over. My name will be Jewel," she beamed.

"Ahhh, Jewel! That's a befitting name! From this very moment and beyond, my Jewel—and *Queen* of the Alecians, together, we shall reign over this tribe!" King Stern clasped his hand with hers, and raised Jewel's arm, locked in unification with his.

Applause and cheering echoed off of the cliff walls around them as the tribe members celebrated. All of them except for one. Unnoticed in the commotion, Delpha swiftly dove under the water and swam away from the revelry.

Olivia's face went pale when she heard the sea master introduce Clara as his *Jewel*. "Of all the names, why did he have to pick Jewel? Why not Ruby, or Pearl?" Olivia whispered.

Alistur's head spun to face her, but he totally missed the fact Olivia was stricken by the name. "How is this even possible, Liv? It's only been *three* days and he's fallen in love with her? And made her his *queen!*"

"Alistur, like I told you—I don't completely understand *everything* about the merfolk myself, but I do know they are timeless. In our world, three days is not very long, but for them it doesn't even matter. Do you recall any of the old fishermen's tales? They tell of some who lost their wives to the sea because they sought eternal beauty and yearned to live forever. Their wives actually threw themselves to the lure of the deep, believing they would transform into beautiful creatures of the sea. So… perhaps it's true," Olivia pondered. "We simply cannot compare their existence to ours," she asserted.

"Yes, I've heard some of the tales, but it just doesn't make sense to me, even though I'm seeing it now with my own eyes." Shaking his head in disbelief. "What am I going to do? We'll never get her back now!"

Unable to control his angst any longer, Alistur suddenly yelled out across the water. "Miss Clara! Please come back! Everyone misses you! And they're worried about you!"

The tribe stopped celebrating and looked up toward the landscape. Alistur and Olivia were spotted immediately.

"Are those your *people*? Gemma and Giles who you told us about?" Treena asked, pointing at them.

Clara scanned over the water to the grasses, trying to locate the voice who'd called out to her. Her hazel eyes locked with Alistur's. In that instant, they acknowledged a mutual realization—and confusion. Alistur knew beyond the shadow of a doubt it was Miss Clara. Her hair was most definitely not the same, and her skin now appeared all creamy and smooth in the sunlight. She was much prettier now, and somehow, she even looked beautiful, he thought. Without question, he knew it was Miss Clara.

"No, it's not Gemma and Giles, but they are other people I know," Clara confirmed, before she dove off of the ledge and swam away as fast as she could.

King Stern glared at the humans with resentment before diving off in pursuit of his queen.

"Let's get out of here!" Alistur's heart was throbbing so hard he felt it pounding between his ears. Out of breath by the time they'd reached the spot where the horse was grazing, Alistur bent over, gasping for air, with his hands on his knees.

"What am I going to do?" Marching around, he rubbed the sides of his head, trying to ease the pounding.

"Alistur! Listen to me! Be thankful Clara's alive!" Olivia followed him around, trying to make eye contact with him, as he stomped about. "You found her! Now all you have to do is figure out a way to bring her back," Olivia reasoned. "Just like you did with Marigold."

"I'm not even sure that's possible, Liv." Alistur climbed on his horse, and held out his hand for Olivia to climb up. "Apparently, she has no desire to return to Mont Renault. I believe that complicates things for sure."

Each in their own thoughts, they rode back mostly in silence, snacking on the dried meat and flatbread.

"I can hardly believe it," Olivia whispered under her breath.

With her sitting right behind him, Alistur could hear her whispering to herself. "Can't believe what?" he asked.

"Her name."

"Miss Clara's name?"

"Her *new* name—*Jewel.*"

"What about it, Liv?"

"That was the special name my father called my mother. Jewel. *His beloved Jewel,* to be exact. I miss my mother terribly," she sighed, sounding melancholy. "She often took me for long walks along the shore. She would sing beautiful songs while we looked for sea maidens. Now it's been more than four years since we walked together," Olivia recalled wistfully. "But when she was still alive, she told me many times, that if I ever felt lonely I should walk along the shore and look for sea maidens. I wish I could tell her I finally found them."

"Liv, I'm sorry about Queen Giovanna. And I'm very sorry about the baby too—he was your brother. I cannot comprehend how much it must hurt to lose a sibling. Nor can I imagine the pain your father experienced, losing his beloved queen and infant prince, only minutes apart."

"Yes, it's very difficult for us all. Especially since their deaths are still a mystery to this day. Father always said our mother was the heartbeat of our family. And I agree. I know he grieves for them still, as we all do—including our Aunt Mimi. No doubt, she misses her sister terribly." Olivia let out a wistful sigh. "The Games of Invasion will be especially good for my father this year. Even though he has named Lilian as heir, he is steadfast in his decision to arrange her marriage to the victor of the Games. He says it will be a good foundation for grooming a prince," she explained.

"Everyone is excited for the Games and the extra special festivities this year!" Alistur tried to lighten the mood.

"Well, let's hope Lilian agrees. She's quite anxious—for good reason, wondering who her husband will be. I wish my mother were still here to help her through it—and, of course, to witness her marriage. Father wishes for Lilian to be wed on the same date as he and my mother were, on the very last day of this year. I know that would have made my mother very happy."

"I'm glad you got to spend the years with her that you had together, Liv."

"I'm thankful too, Alistur," Olivia sighed. "I'm sorry. I'm being very selfish. You never even knew your own mother. So, you're right. I am grateful for the years I had with mine. But it must be extra hard to not have known your mother at all. Do you know very much about her?"

Alistur let out a long sigh. "My father rarely speaks of her, only to say that she died during my birth. He looks very sad whenever he speaks of her, so I don't bring it up. I don't believe he's gotten over her yet—and perhaps he never will. Maybe one day I'll find out what she was like, but for now, it's alright."

Before they parted, Alistur made Olivia promise not to tell a soul about their journey to Goldfin Cove just yet. He needed some time to think it all through and didn't want a single word making its way to his father before he could talk with him. *About everything*.

"May I borrow some of your sketches, Liv? I believe they will be useful when I speak with my father."

"Yes, of course. And I promise not to tell a single person, Alistur." Olivia selected a handful of sketches, and handed over the proof of their trip to Goldfin Cove. "I'm glad I finally got to see everything with my own eyes, but I really wanted to sketch the sculptures of King Aquan and Queen Myrth atop the lighthouse." Her blue eyes twinkled with impish delight. "So…I guess these will have to do, until we can go back."

CHAPTER SEVEN:

A Bittersweet Message

Once Clara was safely inside the palace, Treena caught up to her. "Clara, I mean, Jewel—can we talk?" Treena asked. "Please, let me know what I can do to help you. We all want what's best for you."

"Delpha seems to have a differing opinion." Clara's eyes reddened as she fought back tears. "I noticed her hateful glare when Stern made the announcement."

"Don't worry about Delpha. It's true, she has felt threatened by you, but in time she will get over it. Stern has never given her reason to believe she could become our queen—that was simply a *personal* aspiration on Delpha's part. It was never meant for her to become Queen of the Alecians, and Stern has finally put an end to her shameless posturing. Now that he's asked you to honor him by becoming the queen of our tribe, he will protect you with his own life. I can't pretend to understand anything about your previous existence, but if you feel you must go back to your people, we will understand. We'll surely be sad, but we all will respect your decision."

"Go? I don't want to go! Treena, life has not exactly been kind to me. Other than Gemma and Giles, I'm truly alone in the world."

Clara's lips quivered as she searched for the right words. "Until now I've always had unsettling feelings about the sea. My father lost his life in a fishing accident, so it seems very strange for me to feel so comfortable here—I can't explain this, but it's as though I have another chance—in a new life, with this tribe."

"Knowing you wish to stay will make King Stern very happy. Perhaps you could send a message to your people. If they love you, surely they will honor your wishes and leave you in peace." Treena's luminous eyes took on a lavender hue, exuding genuine warmth as she spoke. "Jewel, my Queen, you truly belong with us now—just as Stern announced. If you want this new life, make it yours!"

Clara liked the sound of her new name, and hearing Treena say it gave further validation, and strength, to her difficult, life-changing decision. She knew in her heart that she was meant to be with Stern, and with the Alecians. For the rest of her days, she could live a life of her choosing. But first, she needed to express departure from her previous existence, with resolve and affirmation of her physical transformation.

∾

That evening, Clara took Treena's advice to prepare a message. She couldn't risk another day, with the possibility of Alistur returning with his father to pursue her and try to take her back. And she also didn't want Gemma and Giles to worry about her. She would be forever grateful to them—after all, the Renwicke's had taken her in and given her everything she'd needed during the past two and a half years. In addition to her gratitude, Clara wanted the couple to know she'd never been happier than she is right now. Most importantly, she wanted to express the fact she had found *true love,* and a meaningful purpose for her life—with no plans to ever return to her previous existence at Mont Renault.

First, she gathered and examined several shells before selecting an enormous oyster that she anticipated would contain a lovely pearl, and then went to work. She dipped her writing instrument into a sea sponge saturated with squid ink, and carefully wrote her message on the smooth, eel skin parchment Treena had provided.

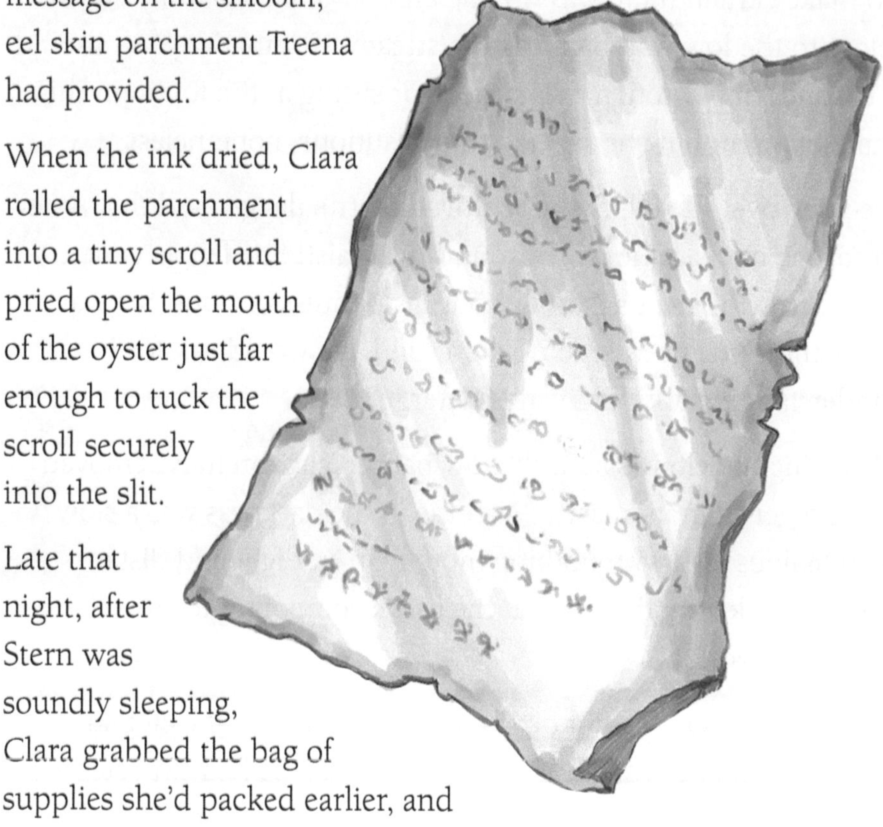

When the ink dried, Clara rolled the parchment into a tiny scroll and pried open the mouth of the oyster just far enough to tuck the scroll securely into the slit.

Late that night, after Stern was soundly sleeping, Clara grabbed the bag of supplies she'd packed earlier, and quietly slipped away from the palace. She swam as fast as she could toward Mont Renault. She'd never swum alone at night and was a bit frightened to do so. Trying not to look at the curious eyes piercing through the dark waters, she sped through the cool liquid of the sea, going out of her way to avoid the scary murkiness of the kelp forest.

Exhausted by the time she reached the inlet flowing to the castle grounds, she quietly wound her way through the royal gardens, with nary a splash. When she neared her destination, Clara quietly skimmed the surface, peering just above the waterline to make certain there was no one around, then stealthily stayed close to the low wall banking the stream. Not that anyone should be wandering through the gardens or sitting at the fountain this time of night, but she needed to be cautious, nonetheless.

Peeking over the edge, she removed Stern's dagger and the oyster from the net bag she wore around her waist. She felt ashamed for borrowing the dagger without his permission, but this was something she needed to do alone and she would ask for his understanding and forgiveness later.

Propping her elbows atop the low barrier, she carefully removed the dagger from its sheath. Working in the darkness was a slow and tedious task with nothing more than starlight and distant torches flickering throughout the castle compound to shed light upon her work.

Clara was extra careful not to cut herself. Slowly, she etched into the top of the shell. It was harder than she had expected—however, the dagger was sharper than she'd anticipated.

"Not bad," she whispered, as she gently set down the dagger and admired her handiwork.

Worried that the shell might go unnoticed, she pondered what to do next. Looking around, she didn't see anything that would help draw attention to it, but she didn't want to just leave it sitting on top of the barrier. Pensively, she ran her fingers along the strand of pearls around her neck, and caressed the enormous gem dangling from the pearls. Disheartened by what she was thinking, Clara made a heartbreaking decision. The necklace was the first gift Stern had given her, and it saddened her to leave it behind, but she believed the sparkling binding would draw attention to what it held, which in turn, would hopefully make its way to Gemma.

She removed the jewels from around her neck and wrapped the necklace as tightly as possible around the oyster, then placed it toward the outermost edge on top of the low wall. She knew Alistur walked along the stream frequently, and she hoped he would find it very soon.

Clara took one last look around, and with tears silently falling from her cheeks, she swam away from the existence she chose to leave behind. Looking forward to her new and exciting life with Stern, she was happier than she'd ever been, but she couldn't deny the pangs of guilt she felt for leaving Gemma and Giles. She realized the couple had grown very fond of her and she knew Gemma was going to miss her terribly, but she was hopeful her special message would at least give them closure and help them to understand her sudden absence.

Wishing her departure from Gemma and Giles could have been different, Clara knew it was best that she should never have contact with them again. She would not be able to explain her physical transformation—as it was still a mystery to her as well. Plus, she could not risk getting caught near Mont Renault ever again, for the fishermen were notorious for trying to snare the elusive creatures in hopes of being led to rumored treasures. Instinctively, the merfolk have an acute sense of self-preservation, especially when it comes to the dangers of fishing nets lying in wait. But Clara was faced with yet another nemesis. She would have to protect herself not only from the relentless fishermen—but from the Grimaldi wizards, as well. For if she were caught, she believed the wizards would do their best to change her back. Needless to say, merfolk are innately weary of human interaction—and for good reasons.

Once again, she entered the darkness of the Azlyn Sea, and shivered in the cool waters—mostly from facing the thirty-minute journey alone back to the cove. She quickly veered away from the coast far enough to gain speed, and could hardly wait to feel the warmth of the lagoon, and the safety of the palace, hoping desperately that Stern had not noticed her absence. As she neared the palace entrance, she rose to the surface and suddenly panicked when she came face to face with the wooden eyes of Lord Regalion—diligently guarding entry to the fortress. Realizing she'd forgotten to take her conch, she had no way to alert the sea oxen to part the doors. Fretting, as she tread water back and forth, Clara was terrified to think she might have to spend the rest of the night outside the security of the palace.

"Jewel?" a deep voice resonated over the surface of the water. Startled by a splash behind her, Jewel whirled around, searching the darkness for the sea master who'd spoken to her. "Jewel, it's me, Stern. Don't be frightened, I'm here."

"Stern? What are you doing out here?"

"I'm here to *protect* you. I'll always be here for you. Why didn't you let me know about your plans?" he asked, as he swam to her side.

"I...I didn't want to worry you—and I didn't want you to think that I was planning to return to my people. I only wanted to deliver a letter to them—for *our* sake. I want them to be happy for me and to not come looking for me. I'm sorry, Stern. I see now that I did worry you. How long have you been looking for me?"

"Jewel, my Queen, I've been following you for the duration of your journey. It's my duty and my honor to protect you. I vowed to never let anything happen to you. I understand why you felt you must do what you did, and I'm happy that you decided to deliver the message. But, I see you have nothing left in your bag."

Puzzled, Clara looked into the empty bag floating at her waist.

With a teasing grin, he added, "I do wish you would have remembered to bring the dagger back."

She immediately realized she'd left his beautiful dagger on the ledge next to the oyster.

"Oh no! I'm so sorry, Stern. I'll go back and get it right now!" She slowly backed away.

"Nonsense. It wasn't truly mine anyway. I found it in one of the ancient treasure chests. There's many more—I'll find another," he added with a dismissive wave of his hand.

“Stern…there’s one more thing.” Jewel touched her neck with remorse. “My necklace. I wrapped it around the oyster containing the letter to Gemma and Giles. I really didn’t want to leave it, but…”

“It’s all right, my Queen. We also have many, many more beautiful necklaces. You can select a replacement tomorrow. Let’s go inside.” Stern blew into his conch. When the grand doors parted, he swooshed up behind her, enveloping her in his arms and easily carrying her through the water.

Feeling safe in the strong embrace of her king, Clara entered her newfound domain—as Jewel, Queen of the Alecians.

CHAPTER EIGHT:
Mysterious Jewels

During the early morning hours Olivia dozed on and off, enjoying the visions in her mind's eye and reminiscing about the wonders of the previous day. The sea maidens were even more exquisite than she'd ever dreamt possible. Suddenly, her eyes flew wide open. Wiggling her toes, she felt no warm lump at her feet and sprang from her bed. "Marigold? Marigold! Where are you?" When she'd gone to bed the night before the cat had curled up at her feet, but now the feline was nowhere in sight. Afraid she may have disappeared again, Olivia threw on her clothes and headed to Marigold's favorite places to look for her.

She raced around, searching frantically through the gardens, completely out of breath by the time she reached the main fountain.

"Oh, there you are!" she squealed with relief. Just a few yards away, perched on the low barrier along the stream, Marigold was toying with something. Crouching playfully, she pawed at the object. "What do you have there, Marigold?" Happy to see it wasn't a fish plucked from the stream, Olivia had no idea what to make of it.

Confused to discover a scabbard lying there also, she quickly realized it looked just like the one she had sketched the day before at Goldfin Cove!

Olivia nudged Marigold away, to see what the cat was playing with. Baffled, she discovered it was a very large oyster, bound by an extraordinary piece of jewelry. As she unwound the exquisite pearls, she gasped at the size of the emerald dangling from the strand. It was undeniably the *same* necklace the sea maiden she believed to be Miss Clara had been wearing the day before! Lifting Marigold from the ledge, her claws snagged on the strange parchment sticking out from the mouth of the shell, dropping the tiny scroll into the water. Olivia stretched over the edge and snatched it from the moving water before it sailed downstream. As she examined the necklace and the enormous oyster, her stomach pitched upside down when she saw the letters crudely carved on top of the shell: **GEMMA.**

Marigold watched intently for a moment, then skittered off when Olivia raised her voice.

"Gemma!? How can this be?" Olivia carefully unrolled the limp parchment, and marveled at the strange texture. It felt rubbery and a bit slimy, but the written message seemed to be unaffected by the water. The words were clear and she couldn't believe her eyes when she read it. It was a letter to Gemma and Giles!

The coincidences of what she'd seen the day before jammed through her mind so fast she couldn't grasp what was happening. She smoothed out the small parchment on the ledge and read it again. The third time reading it, she was interrupted.

"Good morning," Alistur called out. Olivia ignored him, so he walked right up beside her. Still no acknowledgment. "More sketches? May I see?" He peered curiously at the inscription and took the liberty of reading while waiting for an answer.

Dearest Gemma and Giles,

From the bottom of my heart, I thank you for making my life meaningful and happy while I lived with you.

The two of you filled a great void in my life when I needed someone to care for me, and you treated me as if I were your own daughter. I would like for you to remember me as who you knew me to be. In many ways, I have not changed at all. In other ways, I am a world away from the girl you knew.

I shall forever be in your debt and I will always be better for your kindness, and for the many pearls of wisdom you gave me. In return, please accept this treasure to remember me by.

My name is no longer Clara. I've taken a new namesake, for I was destined to live a life I never dreamt possible.

Please keep me in your hearts, as I shall keep you in mine.

Always,

Jewel, Queen of the Alecians

Alistur's mouth gaped open when his eyes strayed to the dagger lying near the letter. Both at a loss for words, they stood face to face staring at one another for a long moment.

Alistur finally broke the silence. "I knew it! She's never coming back!" Alistur ran his hands through his hair, marching around in a frenzy. "What am I going to do?" he shrieked.

"I'll tell you what you're going to do!" Olivia shouted, before toning down her voice. "We are going to show this to Gemma and Giles. And we're going to do it right now, Alistur."

"I cannot believe this is happening!" he yelled into the stream.

"You need to calm down, Alistur. Just calm down so we can figure this out." Olivia realized her friend was in a dreadful predicament and she felt terribly sorry for him. "I'll help you."

"Help me do what? What can we possibly do?" he wailed.

"We have no choice, Alistur. We have to take this to Gemma and Giles, and we are going to tell them what happened."

"You mean tell them what I did to Miss Clara?" Alistur blurted.

"Yes. *You're* the wizard, Alistur! You will tell them what you did, but you will also explain that you plan to get her back, just like you got Marigold back. They deserve to know the truth. They love Miss Clara like a daughter, Alistur." Olivia did her best to be firm, yet kind, with her words.

Alistur clenched his eyes shut, and pounded his head with his fists. *"But I don't have a plan!* Why, oh why did this happen?"

"We can't change that now. We can only try to get her back, so we'd better get going." Olivia wanted to get the meeting with Gemma and Giles over with before Alistur wiggled out of it.

Still staring into the stream, Alistur didn't move. "I have no idea how to get her back. I don't even know how she got there in the first place."

Seemingly resigned to whatever fate awaited with Gemma and Giles, he stopped protesting, but continued whispering into the water. "And the worst part is the fact she does not *want* to come back. Why would anyone ever believe that?"

"Alistur?" Olivia gently nudged him, ignoring his last comment. "Let's go," she said. "They need to know the whole story." Olivia carefully rolled the tiny scroll and handed it to Alistur. "Try to stick this back into the mouth of the shell. That's the way I found it."

Alistur fumbled with the scroll, then placed the jewel-wrapped oyster in one of the deep pockets of his cloak, and the weighty scabbard and dagger in the other.

With his pockets bulging, Alistur trudged in silence through the compound to the Renwicke's quarters, with Olivia on his heels.

ᔓᔕ

With reluctance, and nervous sweat trickling from the pit of his arms, Alistur tapped the heavy iron ring on the Renwicke's door while Olivia stood close behind him.

Within a moment, Giles' beady eyes were peering down upon them. "Good morning, Alistur. Oh, and Princess Olivia." With a sweeping gesture of his hand, and a bow, Giles opened the door wider. "Please, do come inside."

Rooted firmly in place, Alistur didn't budge. "We're very sorry to bother you, Mr. Renwicke…um, very sorry. But, ah…we have something to show you and Mrs. Renwicke," Alistur stammered. "It's about Miss Clara." Alistur looked at his feet, with both hands fidgeting inside the protruding pockets of his cloak.

"Gemma, we have visitors," Giles said, motioning for his wife to come to the foyer.

Alistur felt for the objects inside each pocket and pressed them close to his body, making sure they could not slip out.

Olivia fixated on Giles' hawk-like features, and his long, wiry grey hair pulled back severely tight with a ribbon. His eyes seemed to be much too close together—causing her own eyes to cross as she stared up into his face.

"Hello, Alistur. And Princess Olivia." Gemma smiled and curtsied to the young royal. "Clara's gone to Saint Richarde, but she'll be back in just a few days."

"They have something to show us," Giles stated, with his eyes locked on Alistur's.

Alistur's heart thudded against his chest. He opened his mouth to speak, but simply stared back at Giles.

"Alistur?" Giles urged. "You've something to show us?" Giles' eyes strayed to the bulky lumps on each side of Alistur's cloak. With a quizzical look, he surmised the tattered appearance of the cloak—observing the tears and burn holes.

"No…um, nothing to show." Alistur felt the hair along the nape of his neck tingling. "We, uh, we just came by to see Miss Clara. Because…because we haven't seen her lately…" Alistur gripped the objects in his pockets tighter and tried in vain to swallow the bile rising in the back of his throat. "That's all," he croaked.

Olivia spun her head and glared at Alistur, but didn't say a word.

"That's very kind," Gemma smiled down at them, curiously. "Very kind, indeed. I'll be sure to let her know the two of you called on her."

"Is there anything else?" Giles asked, now looking at them suspiciously through narrowed slits.

"No…nothing else, Mr. Renwicke. We'll uh, we'll be going now. Good day," Alistur answered, without looking up.

Alistur took Olivia's arm and quickly pulled her away from the door. They walked as fast as their legs would move them back to the gardens, and didn't speak a word until they reached the steps at the fountain. Although they hadn't run, Alistur's chest was heaving. He collapsed on the steps and sat there for several moments to catch his breath until Olivia's voice jolted him to attention.

"Why didn't you tell them, Alistur?" He kept huffing and puffing, without answering.

"Alistur! *Did you hear me?*" Olivia demanded. Completely exasperated with him for not coming clean with the Renwicke's, her frustration was nearing anger. "I don't know what more I can do to help you," she waved her hand dismissively.

Alistur got up and paced around aimlessly, holding his head in his hands, looking like a madman when he finally stopped. "I couldn't do it, Liv! I couldn't tell them Miss Clara is never coming back!"

"If only I'd worn my Shield! None of this ever would have happened!" Alistur marched back and forth along the steps, with his Great-grandfather Balthazar's voice pounding through his head: *"Always, always, wear your Shield, Alistur. It will help you if ever there's ever a time the elements interfere in your business at hand—or, if you've engaged in a sincere mistake…"*

"I don't deserve a crystal wand!" Alistur's knuckles turned white with rage, pounding his fists at the sides of his head. Balthazar's words kept coming: *"…and remember, there will be times a mishap may never be understood, and may never be corrected. Thus, it is with utmost importance you are mindful of your activities. I cannot be clearer than this, Alistur: you were gifted with special powers, and you must always wield those powers from the wisdom within."*

"and remember, there will be times a mishap may never be understood, and may never be corrected. Thus, it is with utmost importance you are mindful of your activities."

Alistur finally plopped down on a step, and piled the oyster, the jewels, and the scabbard beside him. Sitting there with his head resting on his knees, he ran his hands through his hair to think, vigorously rubbing his scalp.

"Now, what do we do with *those?*" Olivia asked. "Alistur?" Olivia pleaded, with her hands planted firmly on her hips. Obviously out of patience.

Alistur finally focused. "I'll take them," he answered forlornly. "I thought I could fix everything, but I need my father's help. I'll show him everything as soon as he gets home from the castle and tell him the whole story." No longer marching around like a madman, Alistur was overcome with the realization that he had no other choice. "This is definitely something I cannot fix by myself."

Olivia didn't quite understand what Alistur meant when he'd mentioned his Shield, but she knew well enough that it pertained to the mystifying craft of wizardry, and she agreed he would need his father's help to resolve the situation.

~

When Alistur returned home he found a note on the kitchen table:

> *I've gone to Saint Richarde. Will be home late tonight, so don't wait up. There's a list in the laboratory of supplies I need. I'll see you in the morning.*

"In the *morning?*" Alistur shrieked. "I need you now!" He stomped into the laboratory to find the list Thurlow had left for him. Berating himself again for not coming clean with his father earlier, he grudgingly grabbed the basket and headed toward the forest to gather the specimens his father had listed.

With his chores completed a few hours later, Alistur collapsed in bed—physically, and mentally drained. Beyond the exhaustion, he was apprehensive about the talk he would have with his father in the morning.

CHAPTER NINE:

Complications in the Caverns

Fraught with anxiety, Alistur's sleep was invaded with night terrors.

Trudging in slow motion, he walked in circles, struggling to identify and pluck specimens from the long list. "Coriander, wormwood, chicory, mugwort…Yagg plant…not the Yagg plant *again*…" he mumbled in his sleep.

"Hemlock…hemlock…can't find the hemlock," he muttered, checking the list again.

"…No! Not hemlock! *Henbane!*…can't find it…" he moaned, while tossing his head from side to side on his pillow.

Visions passed through his mind's eye, in restless slumber. Unable to make progress, it seemed like the more he picked, the longer the list grew. Growing and growing, the list trailed to the ground, swirling about his feet, while the size of his basket grew larger and larger, overflowing with specimens. Now too heavy to carry, he pulled and tugged the handle on the behemoth sized basket towering over him. "*Ohhh nooo*…not the prickly Mazie pods!" he wailed in his sleep, kicking tangled covers away from his legs. Searching…searching…mopping sweat from his forehead and rubbing the goosebumps up and down on his arms, his vision would not cooperate…"Four leaves on the Mazie pods…or is it five?…Which ones?...*Which ones?"* he whimpered. He searched and searched, as a strangely familiar melody wormed its way between his ears. His feet grew heavy, getting bogged down in thick mud, as he trudged toward the gardens, dragging the larger-than-life-sized basket behind him. "Lavender…find the lavender…"

Squinting his eyes, he tried in vain to focus on an image in the distance. "Clara?" The singing grew louder. Strumming an instrument, the figure moved in slow motion. Unable to get closer, his legs were too weak to carry him, letting him sink deeper and deeper into the mud.

"Clara?" he whispered in his sleep. "You're alright, Clara?"

Her tone was barely audible. "Yes, of course, Alistur…Why do you…"

She slowly turned toward him, but her features would not come into focus. All he could see of her face were two dark spots where her eyes should be. He was compelled to look at the brilliant green gem hanging around her neck. "…too bright…hurts my eyes," he whined, covering his face with his pillow.

"What did you say? Clara…I can't understand…Cla—" Alistur thrust the pillow away from his face, straining in vain to decipher what she spoke.

"Clara…please come back…I'm sorry, Clara…" he mumbled. Her words turned to garbled gibberish as he struggled to separate the voices he was hearing…

"Alistur?" It was first light when Thurlow entered his son's bedroom, stumbling over the pillow Alistur had tossed to the floor. "Alistur?" Thurlow watched his son twist and writhe in his bed, listening to him rant for a moment, seeing beads of sweat gathered on his forehead. Gently, he tried to wake him, but Alistur's babbling heightened to a frenzy, before he suddenly sat upright in his bed. ***"I didn't mean to do it … Clara…I'm sorry…"***

"Son! Wake up." Thurlow spoke in a smooth, firm tone, not wanting to frighten him. "It's me—you're just having a bad dream."

"Father?" Looking wild-eyed, Alistur swung himself to the edge of the bed.

Thurlow sat down beside him. "You were having quite a nightmare—and talking about Clara in your sleep. Is everything all right with Miss Clara?"

The mention of Clara's name sent a shiver through his body. "I, uh, I'm sure Clara is fine—I just saw her yesterday." Alistur answered vaguely, wiping the cold sweat from his face with the back of his hand.

"What do you mean you saw her yesterday? Clara went to Saint Richarde. Remember?"

"I meant, I saw her recently…and she was fine." Rubbing his face, Alistur yawned. "Like you said, it was just a bad dream. I'm sorry if my nightmare woke you, Father. It's still early, you can go back to bed." Alistur just sat there, holding his head in his hands. The night spent stewing in guilt had taken a toll.

Feeling physically exhausted, and groggy, he felt as though he'd not slept at all.

Thurlow didn't move away from the side of the bed, eyeing his son curiously. "This is a big day, Son," Thurlow declared. "We don't have time to go back to sleep."

Slowly, it registered that his father was fully dressed and the aroma of bread wafted from the kitchen. "A big day?" While he stretched, he suddenly realized what his father meant. Jolted from his grogginess, Alistur threw back the covers and slid off his bed. "Today? It's today, isn't it?" Running his hands through his tangled locks, Alistur looked more anxious than eager. "We're going to the Crystal Caverns! Am I right?"

"Yes. Today is the day, Son. You've been waiting for this day and I believe you're ready for the trek."

"But I thought you needed to test me before we go! What about everything I've been studying? And the specimens? Did I gather the right ones this time?" Alistur shot off questions faster than Thurlow could answer.

"Each and every day is a test, Son. I believe the time is right. Besides, we finished working out the rules of the competitions late last night, so the king shouldn't need me again until the Games begin in a few weeks. So—today is the day!" Thurlow stood up to exit the bedroom. "Your breakfast is waiting."

Alistur quickly dressed and picked up his cloak, grimacing at the sight of it—a reminder of his careless acts. He was ashamed to have to wear the battered cloak on such a significant day, but he hadn't had time to have a new one made, so he put it on. Bracing himself, he headed to the kitchen to face his father, with thoughts weighing heavy on his mind.

Thurlow placed a bowl of porridge and a plate of warm bread in front of him, then headed toward the door. "I'll ready the horses while you eat."

"Wait," Alistur muttered.

"Wait for what, Son?" Thurlow's brows raised with curiosity.

"There's something I need to tell you…and you might not want to take me after I explain." Alistur's face turned pale as beads of perspiration formed on his upper lip. He'd put himself in a terrible position. Without knowing the date his father would take him to the caverns, he'd procrastinated until the last minute to finally come clean about Miss Clara and ask for his father's help.

"I'm listening."

Alistur licked the perspiration from his upper lip. "I've been trying to handle something on my own, even though I know I should have told you about it," Alistur sighed heavily. "The day you rectified my mistakes in the royal gardens, there was one more thing I'd hoped to be able to handle myself. I didn't tell you about it right then, because I was so ashamed. And because I thought I could fix it myself."

"And what was that?" Thurlow frowned.

"It's about Miss Clara."

"How could it possibly be about Miss Clara? As she told us, she was leaving for Saint Richarde the morning we saw her."

"Because," he cleared his throat and started again. "Because, yesterday, Princess Olivia and I went on a picnic."

"A picnic?" Thurlow looked at him blankly.

"We went to Goldfin Cove."

"Goldfin Cove? Why on earth would you go all the way to Goldfin Cove for a picnic? And what does that have to do with Miss Clara?" Thurlow looked perplexed. "Besides, there's some very dangerous terrain around the cove—not a very good place for a picnic."

Alistur stared at the designs floating on top of his porridge for a long moment. "That's where Miss Clara is."

Thurlow frowned in confusion, waiting for further explanation.

"I have some things to show you." Alistur rose from the table and retreated to his bedroom to gather the proof pertaining to Clara.

When he returned to the kitchen, Alistur displayed the items on the kitchen table. Eyeing the objects quizzically, Thurlow took a seat across from him. He sat completely still, with his hands folded on the table, and without uttering one word while his son told him the whole story. The silence was worse than a harsh punishment. Disappointing his father was the last thing Alistur wanted to do.

Finally, Thurlow stood up. "Put those things back in your room for now. I'll ready the horses while you finish your breakfast. We've a two-hour ride ahead of us."

"We're still going?" Alistur could barely choke out the words.

"The day is planned, and the barons are waiting for us. I need time to absorb everything you just told me, so we'll discuss it later this evening. Until then, you have other things to focus on."

Alistur took a sip of the warm tea. Staring at the porridge, his stomach sent signals of rejection. Anxiety had wreaked havoc with his appetite, so he pushed it away, wrapping the bread to take with him for later.

~

From Mont Renault they rode north through Ellinwood Hollow, and several miles beyond Saint Richarde before veering east toward the foothills. Thurlow let his son be to his own ruminations during the first part of the journey. After all, Thurlow was consumed with his own thoughts.

In addition to the bewildering information Alistur had shared, one of his highly paid informants had told him to be on the lookout for a trespasser—divulging that a thief had made mention about gaining entry to the caverns.

Thurlow would go to great lengths to protect the Crystal Barons, and to maintain secrecy as to the industrious jobs the clan performs. He would also go to great lengths to keep the king and the royal family protected, and he had cultivated a trusted group of confidants and informants over the years to help him do just that. Even though information of this nature was expensive, receiving clandestine messages before the misdeeds could be carried out was vital. Of course, the ability to thwart potential threats sometimes depended on maintaining a rapport with individuals having unscrupulous backgrounds.

Even though informants were sometimes overzealous, and often exaggerated the substantiality of a potential threat in hopes for higher payment, it was not the case with Zelda, the fortune-teller. Thurlow had a unique history with her, and allowed himself a few moments to reflect on it. Zelda was the most reliable informant he had, for reasons he chose not to think about just now, and she could be trusted without a shadow of doubt. The information he'd recently bought from her had put him on high alert.

The trek to the caverns would take them across remote territory and anything could happen along the way, but more than likely would not occur until they were very close to, or even inside of the caverns. Zelda had assured him the marauder's intention was neither to bring harm to Thurlow nor Alistur. He merely sought to garner crystal fragments and perhaps some gemstones for his employer, whose identity Zelda did not know.

Regardless, Thurlow knew the poor soul would be sent on a fool's errand, with promises of an extraordinary reward for attempting such a risky mission. He shuddered at the thought, knowing full well if the raider made his way far enough into the caverns to see even as much as a glimmer of crystal, it would be too far, and he'd never see the light of day again. The charmed crocodiles throughout the caverns would see to that. Besides, the trails leading to the riches are quite treacherous on foot, and without a detailed map, or a considerable degree of knowledge as to the formations throughout the bowels of the caverns, an intruder could easily find himself lost in a maze of dead-ends, never to find his way back out.

Thurlow pushed a clutter of thoughts from the forefront of his mind to focus on what the day might bring for Alistur. He knew his son was fretting about Miss Clara, and he also knew Alistur would need his wits about him to get through the physical and mental challenges that lay ahead for him. Thurlow wanted to instill in his son that throughout his life he would face inconvenient challenges—even on his most difficult days. This would be the most important event in Alistur's life so far, and he wanted his son to own it with dignity.

ᔓᔕ

As they rode, side by side, Thurlow reminisced about the beginning of his relationship with the Crystal Barons and decided it was time to share more details of their history with his son.

"Long ago, after the King of Brueland and his forces invaded Fleurbania, they thoroughly destroyed Queen Ruthelda's summer palace—believing she and the royal family were occupying the palace at the time."

"The Bruelanders were pure savages, for sure," Alistur interjected.

"They blazed their way through the country, leaving horrific paths of destruction in their wake—until they were ambushed and finally defeated in the Forest of Bloody Sword, by Queen Ruthelda and her army. But by then, the Bruelanders had nearly wiped out the entire colony of centaurs and fauns, leaving them almost extinct."

"If they were nearly extinct, how did the centaurs become the Crystal Barons?" Alistur questioned.

"It was your Great-grandfather Balthazar who managed to save a few of the clan. He brought them over these very foothills, and hid them away in the caverns to protect them from further demise. When he returned to check on their well-being, the centaurs and fauns had discovered the caverns were full of embedded gemstones and crystal quarries. They led Balthazar through the caverns and presented him with an abundance of treasure they had gleaned, as a reward for saving them. After they escorted him through the caverns to see the riches for himself, and demonstrated how the crystal and precious gems could be mined, it was the beginning of what is now our mutual partnership with the clan." Thurlow took a sip from his waterskin, and continued.

"Balthazar provided the clan with the tools, carts, and equipment needed to make it as easy as possible for them to excavate the gems. Obviously, the centaurs and the brazen, two-legged fauns are the only species with the ability to nimbly climb the rocky ravines successfully, and they're also the only ones courageous enough to climb for the crystals hanging from high crevices, and to ferret out the rare gems from crumbling walls. Even though they've only two legs, instead of four, the upper body strength of a faun is remarkable!" Thurlow shook his head, in awe of the visualization in his mind's eye.

"They trust each other with their very lives. Even though the fauns are the greatest of climbers, accidents can still happen. Sadly, over the years some have perished while mining." Thurlow took another sip, as he reflected. "I think you would enjoy reading Balthazar's writings of his early experiences with crystal, and how it came to be that all Grimaldi-taught wizards would wield the powers of crystal. He was the first to experience it. This very rite of passage today is celebrated because of his way of teaching."

"Sounds intriguing! I look forward to reading the account of his experiences," Alistur nodded.

"And I know you've not yet had the occasion to interact with any of the clan, but you'll find that the centaurs and the fauns are very kind, and gentle souls," Thurlow added.

"Is King Thorne aware of the dangers they endure to mine the gems?" Alistur asked, looking slightly perplexed.

"The king is well aware of the dangers and is much inclined to pledge protection for them. He also compensates them handsomely—along with bestowing the senior members of the clan with titles. After all, they are landholders in a sense. The king goes so far as to have generous quantities of food and supplies discreetly catered to the clan on a frequent basis. They want for nothing, and have no need for contact with outside merchants or traders. Thus, their outings and hunting trips to the forests are mostly for their enjoyment. Son, as you will soon witness, the clan is happy, thriving, and *quite prosperous*. They live a good life." Thurlow grinned at the image in his mind's eye, thinking how surprised his son will be to see the living quarters occupied by the clan. "Even though they are free to do so, I can't imagine any of them having the desire to venture out and live on their own, outside of the clan."

Leaving his son to his own thoughts, Thurlow reminisced about the day he vowed to both his father and his grandfather that he would carry on the inherited relationship and responsibility for doing everything he could to help keep the clan protected.

The king carries the monetary burden of the clan's protection and well-being, however, it's the Grimaldi wizards who've always maintained the deep-rooted, hands-on, personal relationships with the barons.

Even though their species are known throughout the realm of Fleurbania, and they can be seen hunting in the forests occasionally, the Crystal Barons employed by the King of Fleurbania had become somewhat of a secret society, and Thurlow wanted to keep it that way. Thus, it always concerned him greatly whenever he learned that curiosity seekers or thieves had ventured into the caverns—or had plans to do so. So far, these instances had been very few and far between, and so far, none had made it out alive to relish in what they had gleaned or reveal what they'd witnessed inside the caverns.

∾

After several more miles, an unmistakable sweet and earthy scent hung in the air, indicating they were approaching a grove of unharvested fig trees, marking the half-way point to the caverns.

For the next two miles they traveled along beneath a welcome awning of shade, passing through a small forest of behemoth oak trees. Grown completely together overhead, the twisted limbs were blanketed with low-hanging moss, making the scene uniquely serene by day, but quite dark and eerie by night—

reminding Thurlow to make certain their return trip commenced well before nightfall, as the next stretch of territory would be difficult for the horses after dark.

Emerging from the mossy canopy, they slowed their pace and stayed on a narrow path through dense brush for a few miles. The horses traipsed over tangled, gnarly tree roots as they gingerly made their way through a thicket of ancient alders.

"It's not much farther," Thurlow announced, just as he felt his horse lurch to the side. The horse reared up, waving its front legs frantically, tossing Thurlow hard to the ground. For a fleeting second, he believed they'd ventured into a potential ambush.

Alistur jumped from his horse, rushing to his father's aid. Then he heard the unmistakable sound. Scrambling on all fours, he barely caught glimpse of the rattler that was slithering over twisted tree roots before it disappeared into the brush.

Alistur helped his father to his feet. "That's the biggest rattlesnake I've ever seen!"

"I'd have to agree with you, Son. We need to check the horse and make sure he wasn't bitten."

Thurlow examined the legs and underbelly of his horse, and gently patted him in a calming manner. "Looks okay—just spooked. And understandably so." Thurlow climbed back on. "That was close."

"Too close," Alistur agreed and climbed back on his horse.

"As I was saying, it's not much farther around the next bend and the horses will be able to relax soon."

Within thirty minutes, Thurlow slowed his pace, pointing toward a large rock formation mostly concealed by dense brush. "Well, are you ready for this, Son?" indicating they had arrived.

"Here?" Alistur looked around at the uninviting grounds before them, strewn with tumbleweeds. "This is it?" The area was unkempt and overgrown with weeds and tall grasses, lending no indication as to what lay beyond. Obscured behind the brush, the mouth to the cave was barely visible.

"This is just the entrance to the cave, occupied by the clan. It's their living quarters. The caverns are around back, but also well hidden from onlookers."

"I'm ready," Alistur answered. However, his response betrayed his confidence.

~

Rudy, the muscular leader of the Crystal Barons emerged first, with the gait of a seasoned and confident leader. The centaur's chiseled torso and arms were that of a hard-working commander. Other than the grey whispers around his temples, the brunette mane of hair atop his head almost matched the lower half of his dark brown coat. In unique contrast, his thick black tail swished with enthusiasm, and the black, shaggy ruff around his hooves made it look as though he wore boots.

Verah, his pretty companion followed behind him. Her sleek, chestnut coat gleamed in the morning sunlight. Trailing behind Verah was Kendrick, their nine-year-old son. His curious, dark eyes stood out against the fair tone of his skin, while his shaggy lower half matched the riot of pitch-black hair on his head. Kendrick's slightly pudgy face and arms complemented his portly torso and stocky legs perfectly.

Rudy sauntered toward Thurlow, greeting him in a booming, baritone voice. "So good to see you, Thurlow!" He reached down to grip Thurlow's hand with a hearty shake. "And this must be Alistur! Welcome to our home!"

"It's good to see you as well, Rudy!" Thurlow turned toward his son. "Alistur, this is Lord Rudy, leader of this clan."

Alistur urged his horse close enough to reach up and shake hands with Rudy. "I'm pleased to meet you, Lord Rudy." Alistur marveled at the size of the centaur before him, never having encountered one up close before.

"And this is our youngster, Kendrick. Thurlow, I hope you don't mind having Kendrick along for the day. He's been learning how we mine the lower levels, so this will be his first trek deeper into the caverns." Shyly, Kendrick stayed close to his mother.

"Not at all, Rudy. Not at all. This is certain to be a great experience for Kendrick." Thurlow found himself staring at the woolly youngster, thinking he looked rather straggly—unlike his well-groomed parents.

Thurlow urged his horse toward Verah. "Ahh, Verah. So good to see you again," dipping his head in her direction.

"And you as well, Thurlow," she answered with a pleasing, melodic tone.

"Welcome, Alistur." Verah moved toward Alistur. "The horses can stay here and graze while we're gone," she stated. "The water trough is right over there."

"*Stay?* They are not coming with us?" Alistur asked with an edge to his voice.

"You won't need your horse, Alistur. They'll be much better off here," Verah assured him. "And besides, we can easily carry you through the caverns."

"She's right, Son. The centaurs are accustomed to navigating the narrow paths through the caverns and they're much more sure-footed than our horses. It's best to keep our group size to a minimum on the narrow, winding trails. You'll see."

Thurlow turned his attention back to Rudy. "I trust the wagon arrived in good order last night with your provisions?" Thurlow handed him an empty satchel. The bag would be returned at the end of their day, filled with various crystal fragments and powders—depending on what he'd requested to replenish his inventory.

"Indeed, it did, Thurlow. Much appreciated! And I must say, I was excited about your message the driver delivered—that we'd be harvesting a wand today! Please, come inside." He led the group through the secluded opening.

In severe contrast to the desolate outward appearance, the interior of the cave always caught Thurlow off guard, no matter the number of times he'd seen it. The habitat was not only quite spacious; it was flamboyant, in fact. Immediately, Thurlow noticed the look of awe plastered on his son's face.

Alistur's mouth gaped at the sight of the arched doorway opening to the living quarters. Two crocodiles—perfectly petrified—flanked the sides of the ornately carved opening, arching twelve feet high. Their crystallized hides glimmered with a gem-like hardness. Eerily, the jeweled eyes seemed to follow him no matter where he stepped. One on each side of the arch, facing one another, the monstrous statues stood on their haunches, seemingly standing vigil over the colony of centaurs and fauns, with their faceted eyes peering down on those daring to pass beneath them.

Alistur's eyes darted around, taking a mental inventory of the materialistic signs of remarkable wealth; rich tapestries, golden urns, and silver candelabras flanking exquisite paintings, with artistic details throughout. "I didn't know this existed!" he finally exclaimed.

"It doesn't, Son." Thurlow made eye contact with him and winked, making certain Alistur acknowledged his meaning.

"But where did…" Alistur was cut off before he could ask where it all came from.

"Gifts from the king, Son. When we leave here, you will forget about all of this. Understand?"

Alistur understood exactly, but he continued to look around while his father and Rudy talked.

"Each time I have the pleasure of visiting, I'm more impressed with what you've done with the place, my friend." Thurlow glanced about. "And to think, this was once just an *ordinary* cave!" he chuckled.

"And we are forever indebted and grateful to the king for giving us a better existence than we could ever have imagined. It's obviously more than we need," Rudy stated, with slight embarrassment.

"As barons, you're entitled to live like this. And deservingly so," Thurlow informed him. "We are indeed fortunate to have such a generous king. Besides, it makes him proud to bestow such gifts."

Going from room to room throughout the prodigious space, Kendrick trailed along behind Alistur. Pausing near an unusually high table, Alistur realized it was an over-sized gaming table, holding an unfinished game of Scorge. Admiring the uniqueness of the game pieces, he thought they looked more like objects of art, with the major pieces measuring a foot in height—elaborately carved from the rare ivory tusks of the Saega boar. Native to Fleurbania, the massive Saegas are the most feared beasts in all the kingdom.

“I’ve never seen such a set!” Intrigued by the remarkable pieces, Alistur reached toward the gameboard, then thought better of it and put his hand safely in his pocket. “How is it that you have game pieces carved from Saega ivory?”

“All I know is the tusks were found at the bottom of a pit nearby and the fauns managed to salvage them,” Kendrick stated. “It was before I was born though, so I don’t know who carved them.”

“Do you play?” Alistur asked.

“Some. I’m still learning, though,” Kendrick answered. “The fauns are teaching me how to play. They’re brilliant at the game! Gustus says it’s good for strengthening our character, and developing skills of strategy.”

“I couldn’t agree more,” Alistur concurred, catching glimpse of a towering figure approaching the table.

“Did someone mention my name?” Gustus chuckled. “You’re right Kendrick! Later this evening you can learn from my strategies against Surl when we finish this game.”

“This is Gustus. He’s teaching me how to play.”

Alistur was amazed by the size of the faun standing before him. As he reached up to shake hands with Gustus, he realized the height of the game table was justified. “I’m Alistur. It’s great to meet you, Gustus.”

"Good to meet you as well, Alistur. This is a big day, eh? We're gathering supplies now, so we'll be ready whenever you are."

"Yes. It is a big day." Feeling a wave of apprehension, Alistur was suddenly reminded that he had no idea what to expect about the events of the day ahead of him.

"What's the most fantastic thing you've accomplished while practicing for your crystal wand?" Kendrick asked.

"The most fantastic?" Alistur asked warily.

"Yes—anything extraordinary?" Kendrick cocked his head.

"Well…" Alistur's tongue poked around inside his mouth as he tried to decide what to say. "I turned a cat into a catfish," quickly wishing he'd not said it.

"A *catfish?* That sounds funny! I'd like to see that!" Kendrick chuckled.

Sorry that he'd mentioned what he did, Alistur regained control of his tongue. "My father says I'm a wizard—not a magician, and I shouldn't perform tricks on innocent creatures."

"Hmm. I don't see what it could hurt." Kendrick looked him over with curiosity. "What happened to your cloak?" Kendrick asked him pointedly.

"What do you mean?" Alistur asked.

"Did you get too close to a fire? Looks like your cloak got burned. And it's all torn. I'm just curious what happened."

"Oh, that. It was nothing, just…just some cinders. From a torch…" Alistur lied, suddenly feeling self-conscious about his appearance, as if he didn't already have enough to worry about.

Kendrick swished his tail dismissively and walked away to catch up with other members of their group.

Rudy led them to the back of the cave where the rest of the entourage waited. An imposing group of fauns and centaurs were huddled in conversation. Armed to the teeth with bows and arrows, they were also equipped with various tools and torches, eager to escort the quest.

"It's time we get moving." Rudy knelt down and invited Thurlow to climb up onto his broad back. "No need to tire yourself, my friend."

Alistur's eyes darted toward a strapping male centaur, named Tyrus, with sleek ebony skin from his waist up and a matching coat on his lower haunches. Tyrus, along with Gustus, the most experienced climber, took the lead. Kendrick wasted no time squirming his way right in behind them.

"Kendrick! You promised to stay near my side!" Verah scolded. "Alistur, I'm happy to carry you," she knelt for him to climb on.

Kendrick scowled, and hung his head, but slowed his pace until his mother caught up to him.

Verah's voice softened. "Don't be a bother to Tyrus today, Son. You've never made this trek before and I don't want you getting hurt."

Scornfully, Kendrick stayed by his mother's side for a short while, but steadily worked his way toward the front again, loitering near his father long enough to eavesdrop on the conversation he was having with Thurlow.

"I'm proud of your Son, Thurlow. This is a momentous occasion for him—for both of you!"

"Thank you, Rudy. The lad is gifted alright, but it's surely been a work in progress keeping his energy in check."

"Oh?" Rudy mused.

"It seems as though he does not realize the strength of his own powers yet, and now with the use of crystal in his hands…well, you get the idea."

"Thurlow, I've often wondered: is it possible for a wizard to be a wizard without using a wand?" Rudy inquired.

"Ahh, Rudy," Thurlow chuckled. "I can always count on you for theoretical conversation, my friend! The answer is *yes!* A wizard is still a wizard without using a wand, but the wand enables a wizard to carry out their intentions with specificity. You see, a wizard is born with an intrinsic gift—but of course, they are not born with a wand in their hand. As a youngster, he knows nothing about the abilities of a wand when he is first learning the craft."

"A wizard is still a wizard without using a wand, but the wand enables a wizard to carry out their intentions with specificity."

"That makes sense," Rudy acknowledged.

Thurlow continued. "As you know, the Grimaldi-taught apprentices throughout the kingdom may not pledge to our Order until they have harvested a crystal from these very caverns. Part of their oath is to uphold the laws of peace and tranquility with their powers—and they are held accountable should they opt to use their abilities for misdeeds—or misuse the influence held within the crystal. Just as the *sword* does not make the knight, neither does the *wand* make the wizard. Furthermore, just as a knight is sworn to valor, his blade defends the weak. Our crystals resonate truth—and they hold energies capable of undoing the wicked. But, it's the knowledge and the power within the heart and mind of the wizard that gives rise to the wizard's being. Nevertheless, as a wizard, it's certainly empowering when you've got the wand in your hand that you know is *just right*—as if it were predestined for you. Even though there are many factions of wizards throughout the realm, this is certainly an epic event, with Alistur and I being the only remaining Grimaldi's in our lineage." Thurlow paused to massage the stubble on his chin. "However, if Alistur does not discover his *intended* wand today, he is of course, still a wizard—but we'd have to return on another day for him to claim his *rightful* wand."

"Those are thought-provoking words, as usual." Rudy looked over his shoulder at Thurlow as he spoke. "I believe I understand what you're saying," pausing for a long moment. "All right, my friend. Now you must explain to me how you became so intuitive."

"Oh, that's the easiest question of all," Thurlow quickly answered. "From my Grandfather Balthazar—the greatest teacher I've ever known. You were not yet born when Balthazar rescued your own father, along with the surviving members of your clan after the Invasion, so I'm not sure how much you know about him. It was Balthazar who made the discovery about the specificity of wielding powers with the use of crystal."

"I don't know a lot about those times, but I will never forget what I've learned about Balthazar and your father, Florian. I owe my remembrance of them to *my* father. He never let any of us forget that we owe our very lives to Balthazar—and indirectly, our prosperity as well. If not for him, we wouldn't be enjoying the blessings of the king."

They shared a quiet moment in acknowledgment of their mutual allegiances, and trust in one another.

Kendrick inched closer. "Father, it is possible for *others* to wield power with these crystals?"

"Kendrick, you need to forget about whatever you're thinking. *You* are not a wizard! As Thurlow just explained, the powers of a wizard come from within—not from the crystal itself. Do you understand?" Rudy chuckled. "You were not born a wizard."

Kendrick gazed around, without acknowledging his father's words.

"Where is Alistur, Kendrick?" Rudy frowned. "Why haven't you offered to carry him?"

While Rudy looked around for Alistur, Kendrick sneaked off, making headway toward Tyrus again.

"I've got him." With a gentle smile, Verah looked over her shoulder at Alistur. "I'm happy to carry him."

As they trod along, Thurlow suddenly felt the muscles in Rudy's back stiffen, while noticing the herd in front of them had come to a halt. With the group at a standstill, the eerie quiet of the caverns kicked Thurlow's senses into high alert. The scent of damp earth and sulfur rose to his nostrils. For a long moment, nothing was heard but the lapping ripples at the water's edge—until a frantic scream shattered the calm.

Rudy reeled backward as the group saw rocks tumbling down from high on the wall. The sight was daunting for obvious reasons. A man was clinging to the side of the cavern on a hazardously narrow ridge, in a most perilous position—peering straight down into the eyes of a crocodile. In a contorted position, the man twisted his body around until he could grasp arrows from the quiver hanging on his back, and began shooting at the pacing reptile. Screaming louder and louder in angst, the arrows ricocheted off of the hard hide of the beast.

"Help! Help me!" The man's shrieks echoed through the bowels of the cavern.

Alistur gaped in confusion, not understanding why no one made a move to help the man. "Father! We have to help him!" In horror, Alistur looked back and forth between his father and the man clinging to the wall.

"I'll handle this, Son." Thurlow slid off of Rudy's back to get a better look at the man. He did not recognize him, but he realized the exorbitant price he'd paid to Zelda had obviously paid off.

"Why are you here? And is anyone with you?" Thurlow called out to him.

"I was hired to come here!" The man yelled. "Alone!"

"Who hired you?" Thurlow called.

"I cannot say…for I'll be killed! Please…please help me!" the main wailed. "I've sworn my life!"

"It looks to me as though you've sworn your life either way, so why not save yourself and perhaps others from the same fate? I'll ask again: *Who* hired you?"

"A traveling merchant hired me…to collect bits of crystal or gems," he whined.

"So, it seems you work for a purveyor of stolen goods," Thurlow stated.

"Please…I'm not here to harm you," he groaned.

"I'm glad to know that. Where's your horse?"

"He's…he's tied just inside the edge of the forest," the man grunted.

"We'll see to your horse," Thurlow stated. "Let me enlighten you," he paused a moment, regretting what he needed to say.

"It's impossible to kill these crocodiles! Your arrows cannot penetrate their crystallized hides. They're charmed to protect us, as well as the treasures throughout these caverns. It looks like you've gone as far as you can make it. As you can see, it's impossible to navigate these caverns without expert guidance. Besides, the gems and crystals are well beyond this point."

The man looked down into the water, and groaned louder. Oddly, the crocodiles' bulky forms were indeed glittering in muted hues, partially submerged in the dark water. While the man tried in vain to harpoon the creatures, his arrows bounced right off. Becoming frantic while trying to free himself from the crevice that had ensnared his foot, he flung himself into an even more awkward position. Wedging his hands into thin cracks, he searched for another nook to support his free foot, while shifting his weight in effort to keep his body aligned with the cavern wall. Grunting in pain, he clung to the rough surface with one hand, while unfastening a heavy satchel pulling at his waist. With the unwanted weight released, various tools and axes tumbled from the satchel, clinking downward, exciting and taunting the awaiting crocodiles. Hugging the wall with all his might, he gave one final jerk with his knee. In triumphant agony, his foot dislodged from the crevice. In excruciating pain, he inched his way along the narrowing ledge, clinging to the jagged wall with blood-caked hands and trying not to put weight on his injured foot. But fate was not on his side. The unforgiving surface sliced into his hands and knees as he tried in vain to balance himself along the dwindling ridge. The man was stuck, and every ounce of his strength was spent. Unable to hold on any longer, he tumbled head over heels, sacrificing himself to the open jaws below.

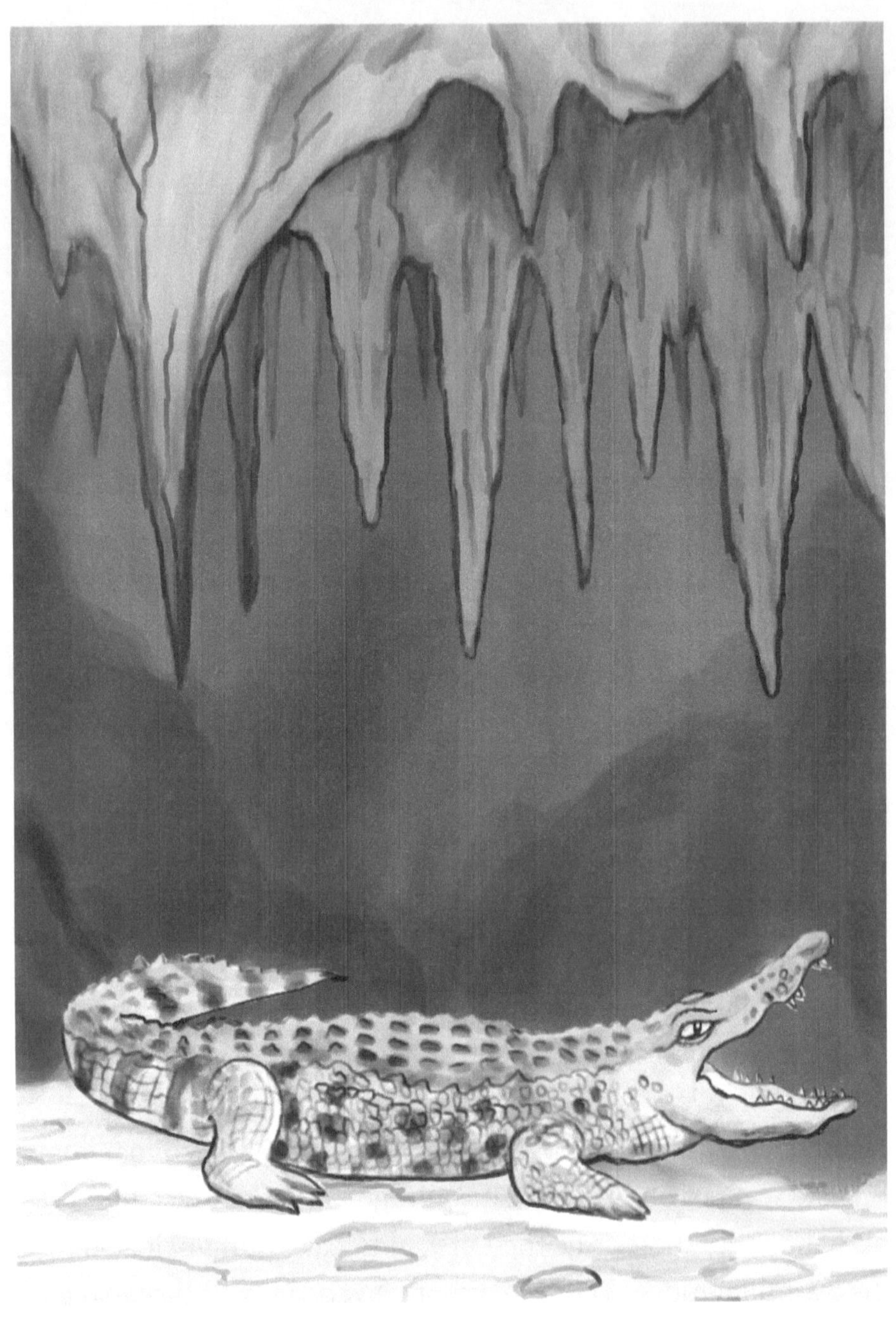

The group watched in horror as the glittering reptile wrangled the man's body below the surface. Beneath the reflection of torchlight, bubbles rose to the top of the murky water, leaving no trace of the man's existence.

This was the first time Thurlow had ever witnessed the crocodiles performing their gory job, and he hated the fact his son had to observe the incident. However, there was no choice. The trespasser had managed to climb along the ledges protruding from the cavern walls, perhaps trying to stay off of the pathways, but had found himself precariously high, and teetering on a dwindling ridge—and still quite a distance away from the opportunity to steal anything of value. There was no way he could have succeeded in an effort to turn around and make it back out. The crocodiles would've seen to that. Besides, maintaining the surreptitious operation within the crystal caverns was a top priority, and the clan couldn't afford to have anyone escape with firsthand knowledge of the enterprise.

Rudy spoke up. "Some intruders are innocent, curiosity seekers—having no real knowledge about these caverns, yet others are hoping to steal away with rumored treasures."

Gustus joined in, "They think they can manage this terrain on foot. But, as you know, even for us fauns, it's very dangerous. They have no idea what it's like until they get in here."

Surl, another faun, validated the comments. "And by then, it's too late. Even if someone had made it to the nearest gems, or even to a cluster of crystal, it would be impossible for them to make their way out."

"Who was it, Father?" With all color drained from his face, Alistur slid off of Verah's back, and walked to his father's side. "Why was he here?" he fretted, looking to his father for answers.

"He's nobody, Son. Like they said, intruders believe they can come in here and make off with some riches. It's a harsh reality, but obviously, they are mistaken."

"I'll look for his horse later, when we're all finished here," Rudy stated.

Feeling apprehension for Alistur's sake, Thurlow knew Alistur woke up having a bad day with nightmares, combined with guilt-ridden memories of what he'd done in previous days, and on top of it all, anxiety about harvesting his wand. Now, his day just got exponentially worse seeing a man fall to his grisly death.

Watching him stare into the water, it was impossible to know what Alistur was feeling, but Verah wanted him to leave the image behind. She went to him and put her hand on his shoulder. "Alistur, I'm very sorry you had to witness that," she spoke softly with a gentle, motherly tone. "I know it must seem unreasonable as to why we did not help him, but that man was willing to risk his life for nefarious reasons, and could easily have harmed us in the process of carrying out his business. We can't afford to have others like him seek us out."

Alistur shook his head in acknowledgment, without a comment from his quivering lips.

Verah knelt down so Alistur could climb onto her back again. "It's going to get pretty rough from here on, so let's save your energy. We have a wand to harvest!" she smiled.

CHAPTER TEN:
More Complications and Uncertainty

As the terrain worsened, with only sparse and naturally occurring formations allowing for light, the caverns grew eerily beautiful. Rays of sunlight peeking through the oculus' reflected distorted shadows onto the shimmering wet walls as the caravan ambled along with their torches held high. The bowels of the cavern seemed to come alive as the group ascended toward glittering patches of embedded gems. Now and again, their surroundings were alight with hues of all variations as small rays of light refracted through the glow of the crystals they passed.

Kendrick chuckled when everyone took on a purple appearance while passing through a quarry of amethyst. Alistur ignored Kendrick's giggles. He was still on edge after watching the trespasser's demise. Being mentally exhausted from the previous few days, all he really wanted to do was to find his wand and go home. He knew he couldn't pick just any piece of dangling crystal though. The thought of choosing carelessly started to eat away at him as he worried about the potential consequences. *If I choose carelessly, the wand may not work correctly for me, and I will no longer have the benefit of my Shield to help me after I claim a crystal,* he fretted. He knew better than anyone that he'd had enough trouble with spells as it was, without risking additional problems by choosing the wrong wand. Taking deep breaths in, and exhaling big puffs of air through his mouth, he tried to relax and waited for the right one to make itself known.

As they neared the next quarry, Alistur noticed a bright arc of light coming from the heart of the blue quarry. ***Is that it? Is that my wand beckoning to me?*** he wondered. His heart pumped with excitement. "That's it! That's the one for me!" he gushed. "I've got it!" He grinned from ear to ear with pride—and mostly relief.

Verah called out to those lighting the darkness behind them. "Alistur's found his crystal! Up here in the blue quarry!"

Rudy trotted up alongside, carrying Thurlow. "Excellent, Son! Which one is it?" Thurlow squinted into the blue.

"Right over there! Its arc nearly blinded me!" Alistur blurted excitedly.

"Go get it, then! Lead the way, lad!" Rudy suggested, stepping aside to make way for Verah and Alistur.

Looking out upon the blue quarry was a dazzling sight. The streams below reflected magnificent shades of blue, illuminated with outlines of the hanging clusters from above. The centaurs and fauns were blue. The air was blue. Everything was blue! But that was the problem.

Once Alistur entered the heart of the quarry, everything looked the same. Each and every hanging crystal was as sparkly as the next. Nothing special stood out. There was no *extra* brilliant blue to be seen.

"So, which one was blinding me back there, huh? *Which one of you?*" Alistur's voice raised to a frantic pitch as he shouted at the crystals, feeling his father's eyes boring into the back of his head. Feeling intimidated, he knew his father, along with the entire clan, was watching and waiting for him to claim his wand.

Reluctantly, he just wanted the search to be over. He asked Verah to move closer to a cluster of long crystals. "Ahh, there you are!" He picked the one near the center that looked to be the perfect shape for a wand. Without looking at his father, Alistur pointed to the center of the cluster and spoke in the most matter-of-fact tone he could muster. "There it is! That's the one! *That* one is my wand!"

"Alright," Thurlow simply stated.

"Okay?" Alistur asked nervously.

"Yes, fine. If you say that's the one, then that's the one. Claim your wand, Son. Make it your own."

Thurlow sounded very nonchalant, as though he didn't really believe his son's conviction for the crystal he'd chosen.

Alistur stalled for time, grasping a few seconds to think it over. "Well, uh, I can't reach it."

Winslow, another strapping centaur from the group, stepped forward. "Come on Alistur, I'll get you up to it." Winslow was one of the youngest centaurs, but also the tallest of the group, towering several inches above Verah. With a thick blonde mane of hair hanging below his shoulders, and a sleek, light caramel coat, he appeared to look entirely turquoise in color as he nudged up alongside Verah so Alistur could cross over onto his back.

"Thanks, Winslow," Alistur said meekly as he climbed up onto the towering centaur's back. Sitting tall, he stared at the crystal he'd decided was the one, but was still not sure what to do.

Thoughts raced through his head. What if I claim this crystal and it doesn't work for me? A wizard can't have a worthless wand! But that's nonsense, he thought, reflecting back to his father's words: ***"It is not the wand that makes the wizard; it's the knowledge and the power within the heart and mind of the wizard, that makes the wizard."***

"It is not the wand that makes the wizard; it's the knowledge and the power within the heart and mind of the wizard, that makes the wizard."

It was true, the cluster had sparked bold rays with its bright blue light, but he didn't know what other signs he should be looking for. Raging thoughts convoluted his thinking. *What if there are no other signs and I pass this one up? What if I don't find another wand today at all?*

As the seconds wore on, Alistur came to terms with his decision. He would make this one his wand.

Perched high on Winslow's back, he urged the centaur to position him directly beneath the cluster. Grasping the brilliant blue crystal pointing perilously toward him, he pulled on it a couple of times but it didn't budge. He then gave it a hard jerk. That was all it took.

The crystal crumbled into hundreds of pieces, showering down over him and Winslow.

Verah gasped. "Alistur! Are you alright?"

"What—what happened?" Alistur just sat there. Stunned, he stared at what was left of the crystal in his hand, while Winslow shook fragments out of his hair and his tail.

Standing next to his mother, Kendrick looked away to conceal the smirk on his face—but not before Alistur noticed.

Thurlow could see tears welling in Alistur's eyes. Sliding down from Rudy's back, he walked over to him. "Come down, Son. I want to talk with you."

With remorse, Alistur slid down, unable to face his father.

"That wasn't truly your wand, was it?"

"I don't know." Looking at the ground, Alistur spoke in a hoarse whisper, trying desperately to keep the burning thickness from filling his throat. He was humiliated beyond words in front of the entire group.

"Look at me, Son. Do you know for certain, *without a doubt*, that was the wand?"

Alistur raised his head to meet his father's eyes. "No, sir."

"Then it was not meant for you."

"But what if I thought…"

Thurlow interrupted him: "You must trust me when I say this, Son. You will know. Without a doubt, *you will know*. Now, let's get going."

With the blue quarry behind them, they soon encountered a stream, separating them from the remaining quarries. Thurlow climbed down from Rudy's back.

"What are we doing?" Alistur asked.

"We're going over to the rest of the quarries. We'll join them again on the other side, Son."

"Don't we need to cross the water, also?" Alistur asked curiously, wondering why the centaurs were crossing the stream without them.

Thurlow's jaw clenched. "Yes, Son. We have to cross the water."

Verah knelt down to let Alistur off before she traipsed on through the shallow water, while two shimmering crocodiles near the shore kept their bulging eyes trained on Alistur.

Alistur followed his father to the waters' edge, but hesitated when Thurlow entered the stream without waiting for him. "Wait! Father!" his voice was full of terror. "What about the crocodiles?"

Thurlow stopped briefly to turn around and answer. "They will not harm a true wizard, Son. But it's up to you to make them realize what you are." Even though he knew this gut-wrenching moment would come, Thurlow could barely turn his back on his son to leave him at the water's edge. All of his senses were piqued and he would intervene in a split second if the exercise went awry.

"Father! Please! Don't leave me here!" Alistur's wails fell on deaf ears, echoing through the caverns.

Alistur saw Kendrick peek back at him with another sly smirk. *He wants me to fail,* he thought.

Frantic with fear as he thought about the earlier demise of the trespasser, Alistur felt as if his face were on fire as the last of the welts flared up. Scratching at his neck, he paced back and forth until his father was almost to the other side.

In that moment, Alistur wished he were home, back in his bed. Being tormented with nightmares was nothing compared to what he now faced. He felt ashamed for being scared and was ready to give up. *Perhaps I'm not ready for this,* he reasoned. The painful welts, thoughts of Miss Clara, the other mishaps in the royal gardens all combined with the events of the morning circulated through his mind like a frenetic carousel. "*It's true…I don't deserve a crystal wand,*" he muttered.

With tears of humiliation threatening to slide down his swollen, burning cheeks, he steeled his gaze on a piece of driftwood floating toward him. As the driftwood came closer, he concentrated on a single thought: his father had told him all he needed to do was make the crocodiles realize he was a true wizard. More importantly, he couldn't bear the thought of disappointing his Great-grandfather Balthazar, and he would have given anything to have had him here with him in this moment.

Alistur looked straight into the sinister eyes challenging him. "I am not a spizzard! *I am a wizard!*" he shouted. With his fists clenched around wads of his cloak, he yelled louder. ***"If you don't believe it, then come and get me!"***

With a flare of his cloak, the driftwood reared up out of the water—transformed into a giant serpent, creating a perfect diversion. Both crocodiles attacked the snake, leaving a clear path for Alistur to wade across the stream safely.

Thurlow had been watching closely, ready to act if necessary. But it wasn't necessary. His son had proven himself capable and he'd made the choice to clear his own way, leaving his fear and humiliation behind.

When Alistur reached the other side, the centaurs were huddled together just around the bend. They, too, had witnessed his actions and cheered for him while his father greeted him with a hearty clap on the back.

Kendrick stared curiously at the red, swollen welts on Alistur's face. He opened his mouth to say something, but seeing his mother's watchful eyes on him, he thought better of it.

Together, the small herd continued, winding their way deeper into the caverns. They wound through the green quarry, then on through a pit rich with shining pyrite, casting a dazzling golden glow upon them. Along the way, Alistur saw nothing unique—no spectacular sparkles, and felt no special feelings. He just gazed at clusters and clusters of crystals and stalactites hanging overhead. They passed thousands of beautiful crystals within reach, but not one of them beckoned. As the path narrowed, the centaurs fell into a single-file formation with the sure-footed fauns, Gustus and Surl in the lead.

Alistur was getting very uneasy and a little lightheaded from the winding trail taking them higher and higher, and he still felt anxious about the potential of targeting the wrong wand again.

"Don't look down, Alistur." Verah spoke to him in a soothing tone. "Just focus on finding your crystal."

Allowing his mind to rest, Alistur closed his eyes for a long moment, feeling a warm, euphoric wave roll through his body. While he relaxed, the calm was eclipsed by a throbbing sensation in his head. It didn't hurt, it just slowly throbbed. Opening his eyes, he saw a pulsating, bright light coming from a far corner in the distance. His heartbeat quickened and the light pulsed in unison with the strange throbbing inside his head. He was compelled to look at it and could not take his eyes away from it. Darkness obscured the area, so he couldn't tell what color of quarry the beacon of light emanated from.

Humming sounds between his ears vibrated stronger and stronger, drowning out all other noises and the voices around him, and sending tingling sensations crackling up and down his spine.

Finally, Alistur simply stated what he knew: "It's there." He turned to tell his father that he had spotted the quarry containing his wand. Temporarily blinded by the arc he'd been drawn to look at, he missed seeing the look of concern on Thurlow's face. Nor could he hear the discussion taking place between Rudy and his father. All he could see was a huddle of fauns and centaurs, with Tyrus and Winslow holding torches high overhead—and Kendrick sidled up right next to Tyrus—shaking his head vigorously, as if he had bugs in his ears.

Alistur sensed Verah's muscles tightening beneath him, as she carried him toward the others. When they approached the group, he heard the tail-end of Rudy's comment. "...we had no idea, Thurlow. We've never, ever taken a wizard this deep to harvest a wand. Typically, we would not attempt to enter this particular quarry from the direction we've traveled. There's another way to reach it, but it would take at least a couple of hours to backtrack," Rudy stated.

"Let's take a closer look," Thurlow suggested. The others followed as Thurlow urged Rudy toward the edge of the ravine separating them from the quarry on the other side.

Alistur slid from Verah's back and peered down the deep crevice. He jumped back toward Verah when pebbles at the very edge tumbled into the pit of darkness. "No, no, no…I can't go over there!" he shrieked. Pacing back and forth, keeping a safe distance from the edge, he ran his hands through his hair, muttering like a madman.

Tyrus walked up close to Alistur. "Let me help you, Alistur." His charismatic voice was deep, and soothing. "I believe we can do it. Together."

Verah quickly spoke up, with a frantic look on her face. "It's too dangerous to jump that ravine, Ty. We can come back another day and enter the quarry from the other side—where it's much safer."

The voices trailed off into garbled blather between Alistur's ears. He looked to his father for some sort of insight or guidance, but was met with a look of stoic indifference, offering no suggestion of what to do.

Then Kendrick started in, talking in a scoffing, whiney voice. "Why wouldn't the wizard want to claim his wand?" Emboldened by Alistur's contemplation, he puffed up his chest and continued, while rubbing his ears with his knuckles. "Isn't that why we came here?"

"Hush, Kendrick!" Verah scolded. "If we are not prepared, it is simply not safe..."

Swishing his tail in a taunting gesture, Kendrick paid no attention to his mother. "He's probably *afraid*," he sneered.

Suddenly, Alistur spun around to face them all. Kendrick's taunting had finally gotten the best of him. "I can't come back here again, Verah! My father is going to be much too busy helping the king prepare for the Games of Invasion! We can't come back!"

Alistur immediately felt ashamed for taking his anger out on Verah, especially because he knew the king would not need his father in the immediate future, but he was fed up with Kendrick for bullying and trying to embarrass him. There was no way he was going to back down now. Besides, he didn't want to repeat this odyssey again and deal with Kendrick on yet another day.

Tyrus moved closer to Alistur and spoke again. "We can do this *together*, Alistur. You just have to trust me." Tyrus was not quite as tall as Winslow, but he was without a doubt the strongest and the bravest of the clan.

Speaking in her calm, motherly voice, Verah made one more attempt to persuade them not to do it. "It's just that we never enter the Onyx quarry from this side. If we had known..."

Alistur reeled on her again. "*Onyx?* Are you telling me the crystals over there are *ebony?*" Alistur shrieked in disbelief.

His mind spun out of control. *Was it possible? Could it be that he was drawn to the volatile ebony crystal?* he wondered. Thinking of sorcerers' notorious misdeeds with the use of ebony crystal, he marched back and forth, rubbing his forehead and recalling things his father had said "*...the ebony crystal is not only very rare, it's very temperamental, having extreme and unusual powers held within its energy. In the wrong hands, its use could have dire consequences. However, when used wisely, and by a powerful wizard, it holds tremendous virtue and vigor, and is perhaps the only method to reverse some of the most hideous misdeeds cast by sorcery...*" He also recalled just recently how his father had told him *"You should hope you never need to use the ebony."*

"What should I do, Father? It's ebony! You hoped I'd never need to use it! Why am I to wield the ebony?" Wild-eyed, Alistur pleaded for answers.

"Don't be frightened, Son. If you are fortunate enough to be beckoned by the highest calling of the ebony, then it's yours to rightfully claim—and it will be up to you to command it. My statement only meant that I hope you never find yourself face-to-face against an ebony-wielding sorcerer with ill intent. Indeed, the ebony is rare. And it is temperamental. But remember: It's the knowledge and the power within the heart and mind of the wizard that makes the wizard," Thurlow affirmed.

His father's statement from earlier that day wormed its way to his brain again: ***"You must trust me when I say this, Son. You will know. Without a doubt, you will know."***

Alistur clutched his Shield, grasping for a shred of inspiration. A voice of encouragement made its way through the chaos and synchronized with the rhythm throbbing in his head. Kind and undaunted, Balthazar's resolute words became forefront in his mind: *"Let not fear be your guiding force. Claim what is rightfully yours, Alistur."* In that moment Alistur felt a powerful headiness as he massaged the Shield, tracing the distinct outline of the fox with the tips of his fingers, murmuring the mantra under his breath *"One who will use all that he may possess of wisdom and wit, in his own defense…"* This was all the inspiration Alistur needed to muster his courage.

"Let not fear be your guiding force.
Claim what is rightfully yours,
Alistur."

Making eye contact with his father, Alistur stopped marching. With steadfast assertiveness, he announced his decision: "I have no choice—I'm going to claim it!"

Rudy's forehead creased. Taking a few steps closer to Thurlow, Rudy spoke up. "Thurlow, you know Tyrus very well. He's the best there is. If any one of them can do this, it's Tyrus." With one brow arching, Rudy directed a comment to the swarthy centaur. "It will be alright Tyrus. I know it will."

Verah turned her head to conceal a shudder.

With Thurlow's nod in agreement, Tyrus knelt down so Alistur could climb up onto his broad back.

The throbbing light became brighter and the palpitation Alistur felt inside his head became a glorious, spellbinding cadence—a vibration he assumed everyone could sense. Alistur blinked hard and shut his eyes tightly for a long moment to escape the intensity of the light, but somehow the brightness still seeped through the backs of his eyelids.

Watching Alistur from a safe distance, Kendrick rocked to and fro rhythmically, mesmerized by the spectacular event unfolding.

With Alistur firmly in place on his back, Tyrus cautiously stepped backward down the narrow path, placing one hoof behind the other—making way for a good running start.

Atop the massive centaur, securely in place when Tyrus reared up, feeling the rhythm pulsing through his body and *knowing* that his wand was there to be claimed, Alistur embraced the moment with his whole being. When Tyrus' front legs touched the ground again, Alistur felt the full force of the centaur's sinewy frame unleash beneath him. Tyrus careened down the path with clods of dirt flying from his hooves, and Alistur's arms wrapped tightly around his waist. As the centaur's colossal body stretched out high above the ravine, with his long black mane of hair whipping in the wind and Alistur's cloak flapping behind, they portrayed a majestic sight to behold.

Alistur squeezed his eyes shut and didn't open them until Tyrus' four hooves met the earth on the other side. Alistur didn't hear the applauding cheers over the other sounds going on inside his head.

Unable to recognize the exact location of the beckoning that Alistur experienced, Tyrus followed Alistur's subtle nudges directing him to the lightning bright crystal. He positioned himself directly beneath the brilliant cluster, as beads of perspiration glistened on the bulging masses of muscle in his chest and arms, with his body shimmering as dark as the crystal they sought.

Stretching to reach the cluster, Alistur pulled his feet beneath him to stand up on Tyrus' brawny shoulders. With the centaur's steely arms holding him steady, Alistur reached toward the cluster to see if he could touch it, then looked down to Tyrus for last-second encouragement.

"You can do it, Alistur! Take your wand!" Tyrus' reassuring voice left no room for hesitation.

Alistur slowly reached, and carefully pulled. The crystal stayed firm in its place. He slowly wrapped his hand around it, feeling a prickling sensation being absorbed through the palm of his hand. With a sturdy grasp on the crystal, he gave a hearty tug. It complied, with a shower of particles raining down upon them. Waiting to see if it had crumbled in his hand, he balanced on Tyrus' shoulders for a long moment, staring at the dazzling formation held captive in his hand. It didn't crumble. Far from it. It was solid! It was perfect—and it was his! He sat back down, admiring the crystal while Tyrus turned around to defy the depths of the ravine again. Alistur kept his eyes wide open this time. Clutching Tyrus with one hand and the crystal tightly in the other, he waved his wand victoriously above his head as they took flight across the abyss once again.

By the time they touched ground on the other side, the pulsating light from the crystal wand had diminished, but not before illuminating a tear of triumph as it slipped from Thurlow's eye. His son was victorious, and it was the proudest moment in Thurlow's life.

Alistur stayed atop Tyrus for a long moment. He was soaking in the realization of what Tyrus had just accomplished for him—without killing them both in the process. Quietly, he slid off of Tyrus' back so he could look the valiant centaur in the eyes. There weren't adequate words to express the gratitude Alistur felt, as he reached up to clasp hands with Tyrus. His small hand dwarfed in the centaur's massive palm. "I could not have done this without you, Tyrus." Alistur spoke with a deep sincerity. "It was *my* quest, but you risked your own life for me to accomplish it. I'm privileged to be in your debt."

"It's my honor to be part of this remarkable occasion, Alistur." Tyrus ran his hands vigorously through his mane of hair and swished his tail to shake out particles of crystal that had fallen upon him. "Each and every day while mining the caverns, we're reminded that we can achieve great things—by working together," Tyrus declared, with a warm smile.

"I must say, that was certainly a first!" Rudy proclaimed with hearty clapping.

"Amazing." Kendrick's comment under his breath was laced with jealous sarcasm—earning him a harsh look from Rudy. With his tail curled around his behind, Kendrick quickly wedged himself between Winslow and his mother.

Alistur heard Kendrick's comment, but ignored it. He was still basking in the exhilarating performance he'd just experienced. In the back of his mind he'd already figured out the probable reasoning for Kendrick's attitude toward him. After watching Kendrick sidle up as close as possible next to Tyrus throughout the day, and seeing the way Kendrick looked up to him with awe, it only made sense that Kendrick would be jealous of any interaction between Alistur and Tyrus—and especially the attention lavished upon them after accomplishing such a feat together. But it was over now, and that should put an end to Kendrick's need for juvenile sarcasm, he decided.

ᔓᔕ

The group gingerly retreated in single-file, with a cool, howling wind ushering them away from the quarries and down through the bowels of the caverns. The herd made the harrowing descent in silence, with everyone indulged in private thoughts. Once again, the caverns were eerily quiet, other than the sound of steady hoof steps, whistling winds, and the ripples of water flowing through the streams.

When the exit from the cavern was in sight, Rudy spoke quietly to Thurlow. "I'm quite curious about something, my friend. Is there a reason you did not seem unnerved or surprised in the least when the trespasser showed up this morning?"

Reflecting back to the incident, Thurlow calmly replied, "Oh, I wasn't surprised at all, Rudy." Thurlow rubbed his chin. "In fact, I expected him."

Rudy stopped in his tracks, looking back over his shoulder toward Thurlow to make sure he heard him correctly. "*You expected him?* You knew someone would gain entry to the caverns today?" Rudy's eyes narrowed as the comment registered with him, curious how it could be that Thurlow had expected a trespasser.

"Yes," Thurlow nodded.

"How would you know that? No one knew of the day you chose for this journey—not even Alistur. And the encrypted message delivered to me last night was securely sealed when I opened it."

Looking him directly in the eyes, Thurlow answered, "Because it was foretold."

"By whom?" Rudy implored.

"A fortune-teller."

Rudy gasped. "A clairvoyant? You believe in foretelling?"

"I do now," Thurlow said, clenching his jaw.

After a long moment, Rudy had other questions. "What are your thoughts about Alistur being called to the ebony crystal?"

"Tell you the truth Rudy, it could be quite consequential during his lifetime. As you know, my son is the first wizard in all the kingdom to claim the ebony from these caverns. Thus far, in my thirty-nine years, I've not had much need for black crystal, other than minor uses in the powder form. Although, we realize it's the weapon of choice in a sorcerer's arsenal—and I'd surely hate to have it wielded against me." Thurlow rolled his shoulders back and stretched the muscles along his spine. "Just as I informed Alistur this morning, each and every day is a test and I will not always be at his side. His reactions to the tests put before him and the resulting consequences are completely up to him. Only time will tell, my friend. Only time will tell."

They trudged along in silence for the next several minutes, winding down from the day's odyssey. Rudy lightened the mood as they neared the exit. "Well, we've certainly had a successful day! I've been wondering, how are the preparations for this years' Games of Invasion coming along?"

"The details have been all-consuming, Rudy. With this year marking the fortieth anniversary of the Invasion, it's been a bit more work than typical of the years past, with the extra events in the mix. Just last night we finalized the rules of the competitions. Now we have a few weeks before the knights will descend upon the compound. The entire week of competition is sure to be momentous, considering what's at stake for the victor," Thurlow declared. "And the subsequent festivities will be grand, of course!"

"Can you imagine? One Fleurbanian knight will earn the hand in marriage to a princess—the one first in line for succession to the throne! Think of it!" Rudy shook his head. "It's quite hard to fathom."

"Because of our alliance, the victor could very well be a knight from Persicoh."

"Oh?" Rudy's brows raised in astonishment.

"With the king's cousin, Madelaine, married to the heir of Persicoh, he's petitioned the Persic knights to compete as well."

"The gesture will certainly make things interesting," Rudy nodded.

"One thing's for certain, it's sure to be a fierce and brutal battle to the very end. I might remind you to make sure the clan stays clear of the Forest of Bloody Sword during the week of competition. As you know, it won't be safe at that time for anyone to be milling about anywhere near the forest while the knights are competing," Thurlow concluded.

"Until next time, my friend." Rudy returned Thurlow's satchel—bulging with the items Thurlow had requested earlier that morning.

"There's something more I'd like to discuss in private, Rudy."

Thurlow led him a short distance away, out of earshot of the others. "Have you ever ventured to Goldfin Cove?" Thurlow asked. "Near the ruins of Queen Ruthelda's summer palace to be exact."

"The ruins of the summer palace?" Rudy looked perplexed. "I know of the ruins. We often hunt the forests nearby, but have never had reason to get close to the ruins."

Thurlow told him only what he needed to know for the time being, and asked him to escort the trek on the following day. "It may not be a bad idea to bring along a couple of your best climbers. I've no idea what we might encounter, and their skillset may prove helpful."

"Consider it done, Thurlow. I'll certainly bring Gustus and Surl. And of course, Tyrus. Are you opposed if Kendrick joins us again? I rarely have much in the way of quality time with him outside the caverns, so another outing might be good for us."

"Not at all, Rudy. I completely understand. It's good to spend as much time as possible with our sons while they are young and influential." With a plan to meet half-way between the caverns and Goldfin Cove, Thurlow bid his friend farewell.

൴

After saying his good-byes, and thanking Tyrus once more, Alistur was glad to see Kendrick was not in the near vicinity, obviously not interested in seeing them off. "Please say good-bye to Kendrick for me," he asked of Tyrus. Truthfully, Alistur was happy he wouldn't have to deal with Kendrick again or pretend that he would even miss him. After all, Kendrick had made no effort whatsoever to befriend him.

Above all else, Alistur had proven himself that day and had accomplished what he'd set out to do.

Alistur welcomed the boredom of the long ride back to Mont Renault. He was completely exhausted, both physically and mentally. Even so, he sat tall and proud on his majestic white stallion, clutching tightly to his prized possession of ebony crystal.

"What do you think about Rudy's youngster, Kendrick?" Thurlow probed.

"Oddly, Father, I'm not sure what to make of him. He seemed more interested in collecting fallen crystal fragments, and idolizing Tyrus, than becoming my friend," Alistur speculated. "After you told me no one else could hear the beckoning from the crystal, I later remembered how Kendrick rubbed his ears, as though he too, could hear the throbbing. What do you think, Father?"

"I think perhaps Kendrick is a bit immature, and is quite a curious creature." Thurlow paused. "However, I also think *you* are very intuitive, and quite courageous."

"I can tell you one thing, Father. I'm certainly glad this journey is over," Alistur sighed.

Thurlow untied the leather cord holding his wavy, silver locks and scratched at the back of head. "Son, the journey never ends. Let's go home and get some rest. I'll discuss tomorrow's plans with you in the morning."

CHAPTER ELEVEN:
In the Eye of the Storm

The next morning the group reconvened near Westridge Trail and headed to Goldfin Cove.

By mid-morning the palace ruins were in sight, accentuated by a full sun. Without a breeze and not a cloud in the sky, the day promised to be a scorcher. Thurlow gazed at the immense, historical prominence. Resplendent with Fleurbanian craftsmanship, the palace had been quite impressive in its day. Seeing large sections of the massive fortress toppled and partially submerged in the cove didn't seem quite real—more like an artist's distorted rendering. But even after numerous plunderings, it had withstood in dignified splendor, he thought.

"This is where we need to take the lower path," Alistur commented. "It will lead us to the lighthouse."

Rudy looked unsure, gazing toward the back side of the ruins atop the rocky hillside.

"Alistur's right," Thurlow nodded. "The higher path would take us to the back side of the ruins for sure, but I'm certain we'd be spotted immediately. Let's convene at the lighthouse and make our plan from there."

Once they reached the lighthouse, the fauns, Surl and Gustus, easily clamored up the winding, narrow staircase leading to the platform with Thurlow and Alistur following behind them. After marveling at the enormous sculpture erected in the center of the platform, Alistur quickly unpacked his father's spy scope and looked toward the ruins.

"What can you see, Son?" Thurlow asked, leaning over the waist-high barrier surrounding the perimeter of the platform.

"It's an excellent view! From up here you can see the path leading to the back side of the palace where I saw the merfolk swimming! Have a look!" Alistur handed the scope to his father.

"Surl, you and Gustus will need to see this," Thurlow said. "Can you make out that narrow path trailing alongside the palace ruins?"

"Yes, I can see the path clearly—until it bends around to the back side," Surl confirmed.

"Even from this birds-eye view we still can't see how rough the terrain is around back, and it could be quite tiresome on foot. Alistur and I will stay behind until you report back here and let us know how close we can get to that secluded portion of the lagoon. Let's hope you can observe the area without being seen. However, if you are spotted it shouldn't be quite as troubling for them to see you—since they don't know who you are, as opposed to seeing me or Alistur. We don't want to frighten Clara by having her think we've come to take her back."

"Understood," Surl and Gustus both agreed.

"If any of the merfolk come within speaking range, I'd like Rudy to make it clear that you've come with a rightful representative of the premises they occupy and we'd merely like to talk with the head of their tribe. If necessary, I'll make the trek over to them. But hopefully their king, along with Clara, will agree to a meeting here at the water's edge," Thurlow stated.

"I'll take one last look through the scope at the landmarks, then we'll be on our way," Surl stated. "I'll brief the rest of the group, and pass along your instructions."

The fauns descended from the top of the lighthouse and joined the centaurs waiting below.

From atop the platform, Thurlow watched the small herd make their way around the perimeter of the sprawling palace, until they disappeared around the back side.

Surl put his hand up and gestured for the group to halt. "I can hear voices. We don't want to frighten them, so let's take it very slow from here," he directed in a quiet tone. "Remember, once they've spotted us, Rudy will speak to them."

"Kendrick, you are not to make any commotion whatsoever," Rudy whispered. "Kendrick? Do you understand?"

"Yes, Father," Kendrick answered, in between sips from his waterskin. "You won't even know I'm here."

"And take it easy on your water, Son. We have the whole day ahead of us and it's going to get hot."

Keeping several yards distance from the edge of the water, the group slowly approached the merfolk, who immediately stopped frolicking and glared at the peculiar-looking band of strangers.

"Good day!" Rudy called out.

"What do you want?" Delpha responded tersely, staring at the strangers.

"We mean you no harm. May I have a word?" He stepped a bit closer. "I am Lord Rudy."

"Lord Rudy?" Delpha looked at them suspiciously.

"I've come as escort for Thurlow Grimaldi!" Rudy stated.

"We don't know Thurlow Grimaldi!" Delpha waved them off. "Please, be on your way!"

"He's a member of King Thorne's court—from Mont Renault." Gingerly, Rudy stepped a few paces closer. "Again—I bring no harm! Just a few words with the head of your tribe, if I may."

King Stern placed himself in front of Delpha. "I am King Stern! This is my tribe—the Alecians! You may speak with me!"

Jewel surfaced, treading water near Stern.

"My queen, I will not let them harm you, just stay near my side." Stern stretched out his arm for Jewel to move closer to him.

"They will not harm us," Jewel declared while staring long and hard at Rudy, her outward confidence betraying the jitters she felt in her stomach. "I am not familiar with you, or the others, but I do know Thurlow Grimaldi," Jewel stated. "Why has the wizard sent you to us?"

"Because of *you!*" Delpha interrupted. "You've brought trouble to our tribe!" she scoffed.

"Silence!" Stern waved his hand in Delpha's direction. "Delpha, you will not speak out again on my behalf." The brusque tone of his voice made it clear that Delpha had no clout within the tribe and had spoken out of turn.

"Now, my queen asked you why Thurlow Grimaldi has come here?" Stern locked eyes with Rudy.

"Does he plan to take me back to Mont Renault?" Jewel asked, as she slowly inched closer to Stern.

"He does not," Rudy answered. "You have my word."

"Your word?" Jewel asked, looking back and forth between the centaurs and the fauns. "Why should I trust you?"

"As mentioned, I am Lord Rudy, a baron, in loyal service to King Thorne. I'm the leader of this clan." Rudy waved his hand toward the rest of the group. "I've been given no reason to mislead you. May I invite Thurlow to speak with you? I can escort him here within the hour. Or, perhaps you will oblige me by meeting with him at the waters' edge of the lighthouse?"

Stern eyed Rudy for a long moment before answering. "We shall agree to meet at the lighthouse," Stern answered. "Within the hour."

"Until then. Thurlow awaits your arrival." Satisfied with the conversation, Rudy nodded his head and led his group away.

Intrigued by the merfolk, Kendrick trailed a few paces behind Tyrus, taking one last look at them. Spooked by a loud splash directly behind him, Kendrick stumbled over the rocks, painfully twisting a hoof.

Another loud splash and then several more. The sea oxen were jumping high into the air and crashing back down through the water with loud thuds as if to scare the herd away.

Irritated by the sprays of water hitting him, and the pain in his throbbing hoof, Kendrick glanced around, scowling. Seeing his father and Tyrus engaged in conversation and paying him no mind, he reached into the pouch at his waist and scooped a handful of the crystal powders he had pilfered the day before, and tossed it into the air toward the hefty sea creatures. "Stop splashing me!" Kendrick seethed, looking back at the creatures nervously. "Wait for me!" he panted, awkwardly trotting up next to his father.

"What's wrong with your leg?" Rudy asked. "And how did you get wet, Son?"

"I tripped," Kendrick answered, huffing and puffing, while holding his ailing hoof in the air. "Those big sea dragons soaked me! They nearly drowned me with all their splashing about," he exaggerated.

"Sea dragons?" Surl chortled. "There are no dragons in these waters! That sounds like a mere figment of your wild imagination, Kendrick. Isn't that true, Rudy?"

"That's right, Son. Those are creatures of the sea—but hardly dragons. They were just playing, so there's no reason to be fearful of them."

Kendrick was greatly dismayed by their lack of concern for his encounter with the giant sea creatures and stayed close behind Tyrus the rest of the way back to the lighthouse, looking over his shoulder frequently—wary of what the crystal he tossed might bring about.

∾

While Thurlow and Alistur stood watch at the top of the lighthouse, Rudy patrolled back and forth along the water's edge, patiently waiting for the King and Queen of the Alecians to show up.

From his elevated position, Thurlow detected an odd shift in the wind, bringing with it an unexpected chill from the north. Directing his scope up and down the coast, he noticed the waves crashing against the rocky shore were getting higher and higher, creating roiling clouds of sea foam. Getting anxious for the merfolk to surface, he wanted to see Clara for himself and get back to Mont Renault before this unexpected storm worsened.

Minutes before the hour expired, Thurlow detected two parallel wakes breaking through the water, heading toward the lighthouse. "Son, take the scope. They're coming." Thurlow nodded toward the ripples in the water and the long tail fins skimming the surface. "Stay up here and keep an eye on things."

Thurlow descended from the platform and joined Rudy at the water's edge. Tyrus and the others milled about near the base of the lighthouse, without encroaching on the meeting.

The merfolk surfaced within yards of the shore, remaining just far enough out to tread water.

"Good day!" Stern shouted. "I am Stern, King of the Alecians, and this is Jewel, Queen of the Alecians! Who calls upon us?"

"Thurlow Grimaldi of Mont Renault—in loyal service to King Thorne!"

"The royal wizard, I am told! And did your king send you to see us today?" Stern inquired.

"No. I've come on my own accord—today." Thurlow hoped King Stern understood his remark to mean he wouldn't hesitate involving King Thorne on a later date, if need be.

Stern waved his hand to welcome Thurlow's words. "Please, speak your mind!" Bright rays of light glanced from the large ruby on his index finger.

"I merely have a few questions for your queen." Thurlow immediately recognized Clara's likeness to the sea maiden. However, she'd grown quite beautiful during the accidental transformation—and now attractively adorned with a stunning collar of emeralds around her neck.

"My queen speaks freely." Stern smiled at Jewel.

"Queen Jewel," Thurlow bowed. "Are you familiar with Mont Renault?"

"Yes, Thurlow, of course," Jewel smiled. "I have…*some* memories from there," she answered thoughtfully.

"And now, you are Queen of the Alecians." Thurlow folded his hands in front of him in contemplation, thinking she did indeed look quite regal. "You say you have only *some* recollection of Mont Renault?"

"Only fragmented memories that come and go," Jewel answered. "Not as much as I'd like, I'm afraid."

"What are most of the memories about, if I may ask?"

"Mostly, teaching my music students. And living with Gemma and Giles, of course." Jewel looked sad at the mention of Gemma and Giles. "I hope they are well. I do love them so. Did they send word for me?"

Thurlow decided not to elaborate. "I thought it best if they do not know I am here."

"Do you believe they will be happy for me?" Jewel asked.

"You know them better than I. Thus, you must know the love they have for you and their desire for your true happiness."

Jewel pondered his response a moment, then her tone stiffened. "Have you come to take me back to Mont Renault?"

"Not at all. I've come to check on your well-being and to see for myself that you indeed wish to remain here," Thurlow stated. "As Queen of the Alecians."

"I do. I'll *never* leave Stern—nor abandon my tribe." Jewel spoke loudly and matter-of-factly, making sure her intentions were understood. "It's my hope we can continue living here in peace."

"I see no reason you cannot continue living in peace." Thurlow's cloak flapped in the biting wind, as he watched them bob up and down in the choppy waves. "Perhaps we can help one another."

"What do you mean—help one another?" Stern asked. "It's the fishermen from Mont Renault who relentlessly try to snare us into their fishing nets."

"I can place a bounty on *any* fisherman who is caught trying to snare merfolk. We can become allies and perhaps engage in a mutually beneficial trade agreement. You can then go about your business freely."

"What type of *trade* do you speak of?" King Stern looked wary.

"In exchange for the protection I offer, you will provide us with certain delicacies—items that are difficult for our fishermen to harvest."

"You are merely speaking of abalone and oysters, and such?" Stern asked, with surprise at the seemingly modest request.

"And the return of the treasures you've recovered." Thurlow's features took on a hardened look. "Along with *ongoing* return of those that have not yet surfaced."

"*Return* the treasures?" Stern questioned the request with disbelief.

"Yes, of course. One way or another, the treasures belong to the Kingdom of Fleurbania—just like the very palace of which your tribe occupies."

"I see." Lacking enthusiasm, he cocked his head to the side, causing the sun to glint sharply off of the large medallion of gold strapped around his forehead. "You are right," Stern paused, searching for wording that would not prompt offense, knowing full well the palace ruins his tribe occupies belongs to the King of Fleurbania. "Although we've worked tirelessly to make this our home, and in that process, we've faced great obstacles and have battled other tribes to keep our place. Not to mention, guarding all that's here from the plundering pirates who still voyage these waters. I've lost many members of my tribe while defending this territory and protecting all that it encompasses is truly exhausting."

Thurlow nodded his understanding. "I see no problem whatsoever in keeping this as your home. The palace was devastated beyond repair, making it useless to the king. It appears to be a perfect dwelling for your tribe. However, I believe troves of Fleurbanian coin and jewels harbored since the Brueland Invasion have been shoring up here. Given the nature of the tides, I strongly believe there's more to come. Just because the treasures are settling below the ruins of the palace, and may not have surfaced yet, does not make them yours. Part of this domain, yes. But *yours*, no," Thurlow declared. "Even riches plundered elsewhere throughout the kingdom over the years were probably brought here, to the pirates' stronghold. Other than adorning yourselves—and quite handsomely, I might add—these items are not essential to your tribe. However, possessing them does make you more vulnerable to thieves and marauders. The coins and gems are certainly a valuable commodity to the kingdom—let alone the sentimental value of Queen Ruthelda's vast collections, of which I'm sure the king would place an extraordinary value upon. So, it seems, you've become the most elite tribe in the Azlyn Sea at the expense of King Thorne." Thurlow paused to clear his throat. Even though he meant no harm whatsoever to the tribe of merfolk, he wanted Stern to realize he was negotiating on behalf of the king, and thus, making him an offer that he really couldn't refuse.

"You mentioned how exhausting it is to maintain protection for your tribe and to defend the territory. Protection in the likes of what I can offer is costly. After all, you now have a queen to look after." Thurlow's unblinking eyes stayed locked on Stern's. "And where there is sea, there's sure to be pirates."

Knowing how the king had taken responsibility for Clara after her father was killed, Thurlow believed he would surely agree to continue protecting her, along with the rest of the tribe. The hard part would be explaining Clara's transformation to the king, and her desire to remain with the tribe. A thought he did not relish.

Stern's brows knitted in contemplation. The mere thought of anything happening to Jewel jolted his senses to the core. "Of course, Thurlow. You are right," Stern acknowledged with a tightness in his jaw.

"However, given your stature as the king and queen of your tribe, it's acceptable to allow you to keep a reasonable quantity of adornments," Thurlow offered.

"*Reasonable*?" Stern pondered.

"Reasonable." Thurlow's tone was sufficient. "What can you tell me about the medallion you are wearing on your forehead?" Thurlow asked. Revealing no more than mild curiosity, he assumed it was perhaps a crest of some sort, but unable to see the details clearly.

"It's a coin—although it's rather large for a coin, and this one in particular was attached to fittings. It was too small for a necklace and too large for a bracelet, but with minor modifications, I discovered it fastens perfectly around my head," Stern explained.

"That *particular* one? Meaning there are more?" Thurlow questioned.

"A chest full."

"Just like that one?" Thurlow asked without expression.

"Yes. All of them embossed with the letter R. Just like this one."

Thurlow's blood warmed with realization he'd happened upon a stunning discovery. For decades, the missing gold coins were thought to have been heisted by the Brueland pirates during their plunderings of the palace, and of course, believed to be long gone.

He briefly gave thought to the significance of what he'd discovered: After Queen Ruthelda and her loyal army had defeated the Bruelanders—and seized their realm, all of the gold in Brueland was confiscated. It was then melted down to honor her, by casting an honorary coin. A coin depicting a true warrior queen—artistically designed and crafted in the highest purity of twenty-four carat gold.

Without further inspection, Thurlow believed the coin the sea master had fashioned around his forehead was more than likely an accessory crafted for Queen Ruthelda—perhaps a fancy clasp for her outerwear, or even an adornment for her battledress. Either way, it was an extraordinarily valuable heirloom that needed to be turned over to her grandson, King Thorne.

"I would be much obliged to have the medallion and the chest you speak of included with the other items we'll be collecting."

"At your command," Stern nodded. His disappointment did not go unnoticed.

"However, it seems you are wearing that particular piece with pride. Perhaps as a token of relevance?" Thurlow mused.

"Indeed. I have great admiration and respect for everything here and I chose this unique piece to signify my position as king of this tribe."

"I understand your desire to bear significance over your tribe, as well as stature among your species. In appreciation for your acquiescence to return the items we've discussed, it will be my honor to visit the swordsmith upon my return to Mont Renault."

"The swordsmith?" Stern questioned.

"I'll ask him to forge weaponry, as well as, unique adornments—worthy of your statures. I can assure you, he'll produce embellishments that will adequately identify both of you as the King and Queen of the Alecians. Furthermore, I'm confident that King Thorne will agree to keeping you supplied with whatever is needed to maintain your safety and a peaceful existence here."

Stern dipped his head with a smile. "That's quite generous, Thurlow. My queen and I are surely in King Thorne's debt."

While they talked, the skies grew dark and the winds gained velocity.

King Stern eyed the wizard. "We shouldn't be experiencing much more than a breeze this afternoon. It seems you've brought along some ill-tempered weather, Thurlow."

"This is most unexpected." Thurlow looked to the skies as water-laden clouds rapidly accumulated.

"Are we in agreement, then?" Thurlow asked.

"We are in agreement," King Stern acknowledged.

Thurlow realized he would be returning an absolute fortune in jewels and gold to the king—but more than that, he would also bring a cache with the highest sentimental value of all the treasures left behind by the admired warrior, Queen Ruthelda of Renault—topped off with a bounty of delicacies from the sea. And after explanation of Clara's transformation, and her subsequent rise to becoming Queen of the Alecians, Thurlow believed the king may even take delight in knowing the palace ruins are once again occupied by royalty. Especially considering the fact Clara will be very instrumental in seeing to it that the Fleurbanian treasures make their way back to their rightful place with King Thorne on an ongoing basis. Even for Thurlow, it was hard to fathom that within only a week's time, Clara, the music teacher, had somehow become an unlikely alliance between the land and sea.

"We should be on our way before this weather impedes our travel. I trust, you will honor your word and gather the items currently in your possession. In three days, we will return." Thurlow gestured behind him to the small herd standing watch over the meeting. "We'll descend from the foothills, where the terrain is accessible and trek to the back side of the palace with our wagons."

"I, of course, will honor my word," Stern answered. "However, there's one more thing I wish to ask of you."

"What might that be?"

"Oil. We need more oil," Stern simply stated.

"*Oil?* Why on earth would merfolk possibly need oil?" Thurlow asked.

"You would be surprised to see the labyrinth of our living quarters," Stern grinned.

"No doubt, I would. But—*oil?*"

"When I first discovered the ruins, I came upon a damaged barrel of oil, with a slow leak. I managed to plug the barrel in order to prevent the oil from polluting the waters. Later, I realized we could siphon small amounts and use it to light the lanterns and torches throughout the areas we occupy."

"*Light the torches?*" Thurlow was perplexed.

"Flint," Stern declared. "Which is also scarce, I might add."

Thurlow slowly nodded. "Oil. And flint. That can be arranged."

"Greatly appreciated." King Stern put his arm around Jewel and drew her close to him.

"There's moisture in the air," Thurlow surmised. "We'd better get going."

"Three days' time, we'll meet again. Until then, safe travels." King Stern and his queen waved farewell, then dove into the churning waves.

~

After watching his father converse with the merfolk, Alistur descended to the bottom of the lighthouse, curious to know his father's thoughts. But it became immediately clear Thurlow had no intention of discussing Clara's circumstance with him in front of the others.

"Are we ready then?" Thurlow asked. "We'd better get moving. It looks like this storm will certainly slow our pace."

Rudy looked about to see if everyone else was ready to depart. "Kendrick, are you able to travel on your ailing hoof?"

"It's just a sprain. I'm ready when you are." Kendrick deflected the unwanted attention about his injury, not wanting to be the cause of a delay in their departure.

"Looks like we're all set," Rudy confirmed.

Surl and Gustus took the lead, side by side, and guided the group through the rocky terrain around the outskirts of the lighthouse. The others traveled single-file behind the fauns. Although the ground further inland was smoother, it would make the journey much longer, and would require traversing over foothills against the blustery winds. Instead, they chose to follow along the barely-worn berm alongside the deep ravine, separating them from the sea below.

Above the howling winds and the roar of the sea, it was impossible for conversing. With their heads down, they unknowingly trudged into the eye of the storm. Less than two miles into their journey the storm turned eerily fierce. Even though it was still early afternoon, the skies had darkened like the dead of night.

Kendrick's ailment started giving him trouble. Throbbing with pain, he soon lost feeling in his swollen hoof. Becoming disoriented in the darkness, he stumbled too close to the edge of the ravine and lost his footing. He tumbled down the rocky slope, coming to rest against dense brush and small trees growing out from the slope. Wailing in pain, he called out for his father, but his cries were lost in the wind. The small herd trudged on, unaware he'd taken the fall.

Rain pelted down, stinging their faces and blurring their vision. In fear of veering off track, Rudy stopped and cautiously turned around, waiting for his followers to huddle as close to each other as possible. "It's getting much too treacherous and it's impossible to see the path! We've no idea if this storm will worsen, so I think we'd better turn back! We can take shelter in the lighthouse until it dies down!"

"I agree!" Thurlow yelled back, straining to be heard over the crashing waves.

"Kendrick?" Rudy shouted. "Where's Kendrick?" he shouted louder.

Tyrus bristled when he couldn't lay eyes on the lad. "Kendrick!" he shouted.

"Kendrick!" They all called his name, to no avail.

Rudy quickly organized a method to search for him. "He must have become disoriented and strayed off the path, but hopefully he hasn't gone too far out of the way! We're going to need to cover as much territory as possible between us!" Struggling against the intermittent surges of the wind, they huddled as close to one another as possible while Rudy shouted his plan. "Surl, you and Gustus will search along the very edge of the slope! A few yards abreast of you will be Tyrus! A few yards out from him, Alistur, and then Thurlow and myself with only a few yards between us! Our linear span should cover quite a bit of ground, but if we don't come across him during the first pass, then we'll duplicate the method with a slightly wider range! Does everyone understand?" They each affirmed. "Let's get in line! Remember, we'll move slowly and stay abreast of one another! We'll call out for him repeatedly! With any luck, our shouting will reach him in between these howling surges and thunderclaps!"

Facing an ever-changing direction in the swirling wind the search was slow-going, combing the rough terrain back toward the lighthouse. The cold wind howled like it had never howled before. The rain turned to pelting sleet, stinging their bodies relentlessly, but their search continued unabated.

"Kendrick! Kendrick!" Surl and Gustus shouted into the darkness, repeating his name over and over, projecting their voices down the ravine.

Through his sobbing, Kendrick thought he heard Surl's hoarse voice calling for him, but was afraid it was only the wind playing tricks on him. With every ounce of stamina sapped from trying to keep from slipping further, he barely had the strength to answer. "I…I'm down here," he whimpered. Then with all the might he could muster from deep in his belly, fortified by fear, he forced one more effort, just in case it wasn't just the wind whistling to him. "***Surl! Help me, please! I, I can't hold on!***" Kendrick moaned. Clutching wet, slippery shrubs had taken every ounce of energy he had.

Finally hearing his sobs, Surl stopped in his tracks, directly above Kendrick. "I'm here, Kendrick! Hold on! I'm coming to get you!"

"Gustas, tell the others we've found him!" Surl inched his way down the slope, moving only as quickly as he dared.

"I, I can't hold on." Kendrick's whimper melted into a whisper. "I have to let go."

"No! Kendrick, listen to me! I'm right here in front of you!" Surl latched onto a small tree protruding from the slope and stretched his body from the core to reach out for Kendrick. With the glimmer from each flash of lightning, he was able to make out Kendrick's perilous position and feared Kendrick would slip away, further down the slope. "Take my hand." Speaking in a coaxing tone, Surl stretched as far as his body would allow while keeping hold of the small tree clutched in his other hand.

"Can you take my hand, Kendrick?" He coaxed louder.

"I can't reach it!" Kendrick's tone turned frenzied.

"It's alright!" Surl gingerly shifted his position. "Here—can you touch my hoof? Grab hold of it, Kendrick!"

Kendrick groped at the shaggy fur around Surl's hoof and struggled to hold on tightly to the slippery brush with his other hand.

"Good job! You're doing great, Kendrick! Just rest there and catch your breath! We're going to get you out of here!" Surl assured him.

"I'm here!" Gustus carefully skidded down the slippery slope feet first, on his belly, grabbing shrubs along the way to keep from tumbling.

"We'll need ropes, Gustus," Surl said.

"Our ropes are in Kendrick's saddle bag," Gustus answered.

"Kendrick, are you in a position to reach your bag?" Surl asked.

"Nn…no. I can't move or I'll fall," he whined. "My head hurts and I can't see."

"It's alright," Surl assured him. "Gustus, let them know we need ropes. Two of them."

Gustus pulled his body back to the top of the slope to explain the dire predicament.

Before Tyrus could reach into his saddlebag, Thurlow had his wand unsheathed and created a small aura of light. Raising his arm into the wind, he rotated his wrist in a dizzying circle, creating a small funnel. After several seconds a lengthy piece of rope materialized out of the brightly lit funnel. With a quick jerk the rope snapped in half.

Gustus quickly fastened one rope around Tyrus' waist, and secured the other one around Rudy, then slid down the ravine with the other ends. "Kendrick, we're going to fasten these around you, but we need you to stay as calm and as still as possible. Can you do that?" Gustus asked in a loud, but gentle tone.

"I'm scared," Kendrick whined.

"Son, can you hear me?" Rudy bellowed. "Listen to me! You need to do exactly as Gustus and Surl tell you! Can you do that?"

"Yes, Father!" Kendrick sobbed.

"You're doing great, Kendrick! We've got you now," Surl assured him, not letting on that his own strength was waning from Kendrick's weight pulling on his hoof.

Tyrus knelt down, as close as he dared, at the edge of the ravine, projecting his voice over the side of the rocky slope. "Kendrick, it's Tyrus! We're all right here! We're going to get you out of there! Do you hear me?"

"I hear you," Kendrick sniffled. "I don't like the storm!"

"We don't like it either! But, it's just a storm! We're getting you out and then we're going back to the lighthouse until it passes! We'll all be safe there! But you've got to stay calm and listen to Surl and Gustus! Do exactly as they say!" Peering over the edge into the black, he coaxed Kendrick for a response. "Kendrick? Do I have your word?"

"You have my word!" Kendrick grunted.

Surl dug his free hoof into the earth, getting as much purchase on the slope as he could muster. "Hold my hoof as tightly as you can, Kendrick. Gustus has ropes that he's going to secure around you."

Gustus patted Kendrick's back, and worked quickly to prepare the ropes. "You're doing great, Kendrick. Just keep very still while I get these around you."

Kendrick was near delirium with exhaustion. "I'll never take any again...I promise...I won't," he muttered to himself.

With no idea what Kendrick was talking about, Surl spoke to him in a soothing voice, but loud enough for him to hear. "Kendrick, save your energy. You need to hold on to my leg as tightly as you can. That's all you have to do right now."

Gustus expertly fastened the ropes around Kendrick's waist. "I've got two ropes around you, Kendrick. One is attached to your father, and the other to Tyrus." Thunderclaps drowned out his voice, and he could feel Kendrick shuddering. When the thunder subsided, he repeated what he'd just said. "And, you know they will not let you down," Gustus spoke very calmly. "You know that, right?"

"Yes, I know it," Kendrick answered with his voice cracking.

Gustus maneuvered into a position where he could look Kendrick in the eyes. "We will not let *anything* happen to you, Kendrick. Are you ready?"

"I'm ready, Gustus." Kendrick nodded his head, causing a pool of blood above his brow to drip along the side of his eye.

"Surl, tell them you'll give a tug on the count of three, and pull with all they've got!" Gustus directed. "I'll get in position to push him from behind."

"One! Two! Threee! *Pull!*" Surl shouted at the top of his lungs.

With his body being pulled, Kendrick swayed back and forth perilously, trying to keep his weight off of his ailing hoof and grappling to secure a foothold in the slippery mud. While Surl held on to the ropes tied around his waist to keep him steady, Gustus worked in an awkward position behind him.

"Come on, Son! That's it!" Rudy shouted.

Kendrick cried out in pain when his ailing hoof gave out again, causing him to lose his balance. His legs collapsed beneath him, suddenly pushing Gustus off balance. Gustus fell backward, knocking himself unconscious. While Kendrick clamored to get on his legs again, Gustus' limp body tumbled toward the crashing waves at the bottom of the ravine, unseen by the rescuers.

"He's up!" Surl shouted. ***"Puuuullll!"***

With every ounce of strength he could muster, Kendrick grunted and struggled to remain upright while he was heaved to the top of the slippery slope. Blood from the cut on his brow spurted heavily down his face, mixing with freezing rain. When he finally cleared the bank he stumbled a few feet before collapsing, with shrubbery still clutched in his hand, roots and all.

"Are you alright, Son?" Rudy knelt by his side in the dark, unable to see the rope burns around his son's waist, or the blood streaming from his brow.

"I'm…I'm fine, Father," he huffed. "I'm just out of breath…and my legs are burning."

"Just rest right there, Son. I'll check your legs and make sure nothing is broken."

"You did it, Kendrick! You don't know your own strength!" Tyrus clapped for him.

Surl hauled himself over the top of the slope with a heavy sadness.

"Surl! You and Gustus are the real heroes here!" Rudy exclaimed.

Surl crouched on the ground near Kendrick and hung his head, his shoulders shaking.

"Surl? Where is Gustus?" Rudy asked emphatically.

Surl raised his head with tears spilling from his eyes. "He…he must have slipped, Rudy." Ravaged by grief, Surl held his head in his hands.

The reverie came to an immediate halt. Tyrus and Rudy cautiously peered over the side of the ravine. "Gussstusss!" they shouted repeatedly.

The bottom of the chasm could not be seen, and the winds howling over the raging water carried their voices into unresponsive darkness. Thurlow and Alistur looked over the side, speechless and sorrowful.

∾

The trek back to the lighthouse was miserable and somber. With their heads down, they trudged slowly through the storm, huddled in a tight group. Surl rode atop Tyrus with his face buried in Tyrus' broad back, letting grief consume him.

By the time they approached the lighthouse more than an hour later, the storm had not subdued in the least. In fact, it had become an undeniable force against nature, and it was rapidly gaining even more velocity. Thurlow's senses were piqued and the niggling feeling he'd felt since the storm came up intensified. Something was very wrong. Out in the distance, through the scope, he surveyed light—*shining brightly over calm seas*—in strange contrast to the roiling water and the pitch darkness looming around the lighthouse. In addition, the storm was impossibly cold. Even in the twilight of winter, which was at least three months away, the temperatures in the kingdom rarely turn bitterly cold. To the contrary, summers were long and the winter months were mild throughout most parts of Fleurbania. Only in the most northern, mountainous parts of the kingdom did the temperatures turn frigid.

Thurlow ushered everyone safely inside the lighthouse then climbed the winding stairs. When he pulled himself up onto the platform, his scope was not needed. It was plain to see that the storm was not of natural causes.

The towering sculptures appeared to be alive, with King Aquan and Queen Myrth hurling their arms about—but not in effort to *calm* the seas—they were *orchestrating* the severe conditions! Myrth caught glimpse of Thurlow and blew a turbulent frosty wind upon him, forcing him back down the winding stairs.

From the stairwell, Thurlow could hear Rudy consoling Kendrick.

"Son, there's no need to apologize, accidents happen. It's not your fault you fell down the ravine. It's just a bad bump and a cut, Son.

It will heal. Let's be thankful a cut on your brow is the worst injury you sustained. And it's not your fault Gustus slipped. We are all very, very sad for Gustus. This was a tragic accident, Son—but it was indeed an accident."

Kendrick only wailed louder. "I'm sorry! I'm sorry and I'll never do it again!"

Taking note of Kendrick's sobbing and repeated apologies, Thurlow became curious. "Kendrick, is there anything else we need to know in order to help you? Do you have other injuries—or did anything else happen?" Thurlow asked.

"No, I don't have any other injuries," he answered in a whiney voice. "But, but..." his voice trailed off into sobs.

"But what, Son? What is the matter? If you don't tell us, we can't help you," Rudy implored.

"I might have done something. But, I'm not exactly sure." Kendrick hung his head. "I...I was mad at them."

"Mad at who, Son?"

"Those big sea dragons. When they kept splashing me."

"But as I told you, they were just playing," Rudy stated.

"Did anything else happen back there when they splashed you?" Thurlow asked.

"I didn't know they were just playing, so I...I tossed some crystal powder on them to make them stop," Kendrick answered sheepishly.

"Crystal powder?" Rudy was taken aback and totally confused. "Why would you do that, Son? Crystal is of no use to you!" Rudy shook his head in disbelief at his son's admission. "Why would you be carrying crystal powder anyway?"

Without waiting for Kendrick to answer, Thurlow immediately returned to the top of the lighthouse with Alistur following right behind him. The platform was covered with a sheet of ice, making it nearly impossible to stay upright against the fierce wind. Arcing his wand through the dark, Thurlow tried with all the power he could elicit to gain control of the sculptures. To no avail, the copper figures raged on, with Thurlow's powers having no effect whatsoever on their misdeeds.

Myrth pursed her lips and quickly turned her attention toward Alistur. In a split second, he tumbled head over heels, leaving him sprawled against the barrier.

Quickly realizing his father had no influence over the storm, Alistur hugged the barrier and scooted over the ice to reach the staircase. Hanging on with every muscle in his body, he slowly worked his way down the winding stairs. Struggling to stand upright he hunkered down and fought his way to the water's edge. Bracing himself against the wind, he brazenly faced the brunt of the storm.

With a glance toward the lighthouse, he saw his father clinging desperately to the barrier. Feeling his strength waning against the ravages of the wind and the deluge of pelting sleet, Alistur unsheathed his crystal wand as thunder rolled across the fiery skies.

With unwavering confidence, he held the wand high overhead, making wide slices through the air. A tingling sensation zigzagged beneath his scalp, as arcs of lightning crackled from the tip of his wand, trailing far out across the roiling seas. Nearing utter exhaustion and struggling to keep standing, Alistur turned his attention toward the top of the lighthouse.

Trying to shield their eyes from the blinding arcs, King Aquan and Queen Myrth halted their movements to slow motion until they finally returned to their original sculpted poses. Within moments, the pelting rain turned to a mere drizzle and the freezing wind retreated to a balmy breeze. With rays of sun piercing through the dusky clouds, the storm had all but vanished.

Kendrick stayed frozen in place behind Rudy, peeking around his father's side, still feeling guilty, as Alistur made his way to the lighthouse.

"Are you alright, Kendrick?" Alistur asked.

"Yes, Alistur. I'm alright." Alistur locked eyes with Kendrick and for the first time he did not see the resentful, smug look that he usually received from Kendrick.

"You saved us, Alistur," Kendrick declared. "You stopped the bad storm!" Kendrick's tail swished with enthusiasm.

"Indeed! I believe he did, Son!" Rudy clapped his hands.

Thurlow clamored down the stairs and joined the group while everyone cheered for Alistur.

"Now, then. I do believe it's time we head for home," Thurlow announced. His mind was convoluted with myriad thoughts and emotions and he wanted to get the long ride home behind him. Although there was much he wanted to focus his attention on, taking forefront was his son's astonishing feat to calm the horrific storm. Undoubtedly, Alistur had saved them from the perils of the life-threatening storm, and he'd wielded powers that Thurlow himself had only dreamt of being capable of. He wanted nothing more than to bask in the jubilation of his son's triumph. However, this day was not over, with another important matter yet to tend to—and sure to be charged with its own emotions.

∾

The group ambled along, with Kendrick walking closely behind Alistur, in silent admiration. Despite the bright rays of sun pouring down upon them, the mood was somber as everyone was quiet in mournful contemplation of their own thoughts about the events of the day.

Slumped in grief atop the back of Tyrus, Surl suddenly bristled. Catching sight of what appeared to be a mound of fur propped against a tree, Surl sat up straight, squinting his eyes in the sun to get a better look. "Stop! Tyrus, stop!" Surl jumped off Tyrus' back. "It's Gustus! Oh, Gustus! I can't believe it!" Surl knelt down beside his friend. "*You're alive!*"

Gustus was delirious from pain and could barely open his eyes. "I can't. I can't move. Please…go on without me." Exhausted beyond the desire to recover, his voice was barely more than a guttural whisper.

"Gustus, listen to me. We're going to take you home! You are going to be alright!"

"Surl is right. We're here for you." Rudy knelt down on the other side of him.

"I…I can't walk. There's too much pain," Gustus whimpered. "Please…just go. Save yourselves."

"Gustus, we're all safe now. Your leg is broken, but you don't have to walk on it. We're going to get you home and then we'll tend to your leg," Rudy assured him.

"Here, have a few sips of water," Surl held out his waterskin.

Unable to grasp, Gustus let it fall from his quivering, blood-caked hands. The climb up the ravine had taken a merciless toll on his arms and knees. The muscles in his upper body could do no more.

Surl patted his friend gently and held the water to Gustus' lips, noticing the severe cuts and scrapes on his hands and forearms. "Please, take some water. We're heading home, my friend."

Gustus managed a couple of small sips, then slumped back against the tree, with blood dripping from the back of his head.

Surl put the water down and helped Gustus remain upright. "You've lost a lot of blood from that nasty gash. I need something to wrap around your head to minimize the bleeding."

Alistur quickly ripped a portion of fabric from his cloak and handed it to Surl. "I need a new one anyway," he asserted.

"You gave me quite a scare, Gustus," Surl murmured, as he gently wrapped the fabric around Gustus' head.

"I gave myself quite a scare. I only wish I could remember what happened."

"You don't recall what happened?" Surl asked.

"The last thing I remember is almost drowning in freezing water at the bottom of…I don't know where…in the dark of night. So, I really don't know how many days I've been sitting against this tree." He took a deep breath before finishing his thought. "My leg is broken and I do know it was taking more strength than I had to fight the current and climb a rocky slope to get here…but I guess I made it…because here I sit." He chuckled slightly, but the talking depleted his energy.

"You've the strength of an ogre—and perhaps just as stubborn, too. And I'm glad for it, my friend." Surl patted him again. "I'm sure it's hard to believe this, but it happened just a few hours ago.

We'll talk about it all later, once you've regained your strength. But for now, we're going to get you warmed up and hydrated. You're suffering with hypothermia."

Tyrus knelt down. "Put him up here between us, so you can keep him astride. I can carry you both." Surl lifted his friend and carefully placed him on Tyrus' back, then climbed on behind him, with plenty of room for both of them on the centaur's powerful frame.

"I hope the trek is not too painful for you, my friend. We'll take it as easy as possible. Just rest the best you can. All you have to do is stay awake until we can treat that wound on the back of your head. You can sleep all you want after that," Surl advised.

"Sleep? From what I can recall, we've an unfinished game of Scorge waiting on the table for us. And I believe I was winning," Gustus retorted with a raspy chuckle.

"Winning? From what I recall, you'd lost so many pieces I thought you'd forfeited that game!" Surl teased.

"We'll see about that," Gustus answered with a sly grin.

"Indeed, we will," Surl patted him on the back with a big sigh of relief, knowing his friend was going to be alright. "Indeed, we will."

∾

The rest of the trek was uneventful, but joyful, knowing their dear friend was not mortally harmed, giving Thurlow time to ruminate about the day's events. And an important revelation. Although there was still concern for Gustus' well-being, the moods were much lighter.

As they neared the fork in the road, which would lead the centaurs toward the caverns, Thurlow slowed his pace and decided to speak his mind. "While the events throughout the day caused us much concern and a near misfortune, it has ended with cause to celebrate."

Thurlow sidled up alongside Kendrick and Alistur, bringing his horse to a halt in front of them. "Kendrick, what do you say you hand over the remaining crystal in your pouch to Alistur?"

Confused, and slightly annoyed at the suggestion, Kendrick took a step toward his father with his tail between his legs.

Thurlow allowed a rare grin to cross his lips. "He'll keep it safe for you until we can begin teaching you how to safely handle the powers of the crystal. In the meantime, let's keep our eyes open for a nice, sturdy birch limb. I'm sure Alistur can help you find just the right one."

Kendrick was speechless and unsure what it all meant, but his tail swished with anticipation, as he handed over his pouch to Alistur.

This time Thurlow directed his words to Rudy. "There are many magical things a mere mortal cannot explain. And like I've said before, we all have a little bit of magic inside of us—but only those born with a true wizard's gift are capable of gleaning from the wisdom within."

"We all have a little bit of magic inside of us—but only those born with a true wizard's gift are capable of gleaning from the wisdom within."

"Yes...as you've mentioned before," Rudy stated, with eyes wide, wondering what *exactly* Thurlow was getting at.

"Before a wizard gains control of his capabilities, he must learn how to harness his energy and develop his skills—such as the way I've worked with Alistur."

"Yes, go on," Rudy encouraged.

"To a mere mortal, the crystal fragments Kendrick carried in his bag would serve as nothing more than fascinating specimens in a gem collection. But the powders he tossed toward the sea creatures carried energy that *only a wizard* could possibly wield. Even though it was an innocent act, the powers within the crystal were nonetheless wielded."

Rudy struggled to find words. He opened his mouth to speak, but nothing crossed his lips.

"I'm saying, Kendrick needs to learn to wield his powers with *specificity,*" Thurlow clarified.

"With specificity?" Rudy asked cautiously. "Kendrick...my son ... a *wizard?*" he implored, rubbing his chin. "Could it be, Thurlow?"

"Indeed, my friend! I believe we have a new apprentice on the rise," Thurlow declared with a twinkle in his eye.

"This is truly a reason for celebration! Kendrick—a *wizard!* Perhaps that explains why he finds the crystal caverns so appealing!" Tyrus clapped heartily for Kendrick. "Wait till the rest of our clan hears about this!"

Embarrassed by all the attention directed at him, Kendrick was at a loss for words, rocking back and forth between his two front legs.

"Son, I am still curious how it is that you have crystal in your pouch?" Rudy asked.

"Tyrus and Winslow were collecting some from each quarry to replenish Thurlow's supplies, and I took some from their pouches and put it in mine." He hung his head in shame. "And I scooped up the fragments they shook out of their tails. But, I see now it was wrong. I'm sorry for all of this. I especially feel awful for Gustus, and I'm sorry I caused him to break his leg. Especially since he promised not to let anything happen to *me*." Kendrick's cheeks reddened with emotion. "I wish I had the broken leg instead of him."

"Nonsense, lad!" Gustus managed. "This was an accident. I'll be good as new in no time. And when I'm healed, I'll be eager to see what you can do. After you've studied a bit with Thurlow, that is!" Gustus chuckled.

Once the centaurs and fauns had parted ways, Thurlow and Alistur headed south. "Son, although I believe I already know the answer, considering the trouble I had combatting the storm, what color are the crystals Kendrick was carrying?"

Alistur looked inside the pouch, then tightened it securely around his waist. "His pouch is filled with particles of various colors…plus, a pile of ebony shards."

Thurlow's brows knitted with an understanding of the implication of Kendrick's actions. He nodded and released his hair from its leather cord, letting his silver locks tumble about his shoulders. "I believe we'd better dust off the Shield," Thurlow said as he urged his horse toward Mont Renault. "But first, we need to pay a visit to Gemma and Giles."

Gripping his reins, the blood rushed from Alistur's knuckles, with thoughts of Miss Clara, and the impending conversation with Gemma and Giles. He spurred his horse to follow, with his burnt, storm-tattered cloak flapping wildly behind him.

CHAPTER TWELVE:

Things Great-Grandfather Used to Say

It was late evening when Thurlow rapped on the door, feeling anxious about how this visit would go.

The door creaked open. "Good evening, Thurlow. And Alistur. Please, come in." Giles opened the door wider.

Thurlow spoke. "Good evening, Giles. We've come to see you and Gemma about Miss Clara."

Gemma appeared from the hallway and quickly interrupted, without giving Thurlow a chance to continue. "Good evening, Thurlow. Clara's been in Saint Richarde to see her students. The coach must be late, but we expect her any moment now. Is there something we can help you with?"

Thurlow cleared his throat. "Miss Clara did not go to Saint Richarde."

Stricken with confusion, Gemma stared at them blankly. "Oh?" she squeaked.

"Where is she then?" Giles asked, peering beyond the stoop, as if Clara were perhaps waiting outside.

Thurlow took a deep breath, with his eyes locked on Giles. "I believe Miss Clara has answered a higher calling for her life's purpose," Thurlow stated.

"A higher calling?" Giles said slowly. *"For her life's purpose?"* he asked, arching one bushy brow high into his forehead, causing it to look like a caterpillar rearing up.

"She's at Goldfin Cove," Thurlow clenched his jaw, waiting for that much to sink in.

"Goldfin Cove?" Gemma questioned. "There are no people there—certainly no music students. Why would she go there?"

"You are quite correct, Gemma." Thurlow took another deep breath. "There are…no *people* living at the ruins…only merfolk."

"Merfolk?" Gemma's voice raised an octave. "Sea maidens? What do you mean, Thurlow?" Alistur stood rooted in place, with his tongue pressed safely behind clenched teeth. His heart rate keeping pace with the explosion of thoughts jamming through his mind.

Thurlow was glad Gemma actually mentioned the sea maidens. Besides, there was no way around it other than to just spit it out. "That is precisely what I am talking about, Gemma. Sea maidens."

Gemma's lips grimaced in confusion. "But…but, I don't understand what you are saying. Precisely."

"I can confirm that Miss Clara wishes to remain in Goldfin Cove," Thurlow stated.

You are trying to tell us Clara wants to *live* in Goldfin Cove? Among merfolk?" Gemma's face contorted with disbelief as she peppered him with questions. "Why? *And how*? How can she possibly live among creatures of the sea?"

"Well, ahh, she had some help." Thurlow's eyes strayed to Alistur.

"She asked Alistur to ***help*** her?" Gemma asked warily.

"She didn't exactly ***ask*** for his help. It was more of an accident."

Giles finally spoke up. "*An accident?*" His wiry brows collapsed into a frown, as he stared at Alistur's battered cloak.

"On the morning she planned to go to Saint Richarde, Miss Clara accidentally tripped and fell into the stream while Alistur was practicing. More specifically, she was caught in the cusp of his spell...and carried to the cove by the current."

"Carried to the cove? Under water?" Gemma shrieked.

"Yes, Gemma. But it was by his spell that she was kept alive—and able to keep breathing. Under water," Thurlow answered in a gentle tone.

"Under water?" Gemma's amber eyes darkened and bore into Thurlow's. "*Breathing under water?* You are saying she is alive... yet...breathing under water?"

"Yes, Gemma. Miss Clara is quite alive. And well." Thurlow inhaled deeply. "As a sea maiden."

With fire now behind the amber, Gemma fixed her eyes on Alistur. "*A sea maiden*, Alistur? Our Clara...living with *merfolk*?" She didn't wait for him to respond. "How will you get her back?

Are you sure your imagination didn't get the best of you?"

Alistur's lips parted to speak but Thurlow didn't give him a chance. "And I assure you, we tried to get her to come back with us. However, we failed in that attempt."

"You failed?" Giles asked. "You are saying that you actually *spoke* with her?"

"Most certainly. We talked with her this afternoon, and our powers were not tested to force Miss Clara to return with us. She was emphatic about her decision to remain in the cove. The lure of the sea is a force I dare not reckon with. Undoubtedly, her desire to stay with the tribe would surely have overpowered my mortal skills."

"The *tribe?*" Gemma squeaked.

"Yes. She lives with the Alecians—an elite tribe of merfolk, and I can show you proof that she is indeed alive and quite happy."

"*Proof?*" Giles asked, now with two caterpillar-eyebrows reaching high on his forehead.

Alistur couldn't contain himself any longer. "Yes! They've even made her the *queen* of their tribe!" He pulled the drawings from his satchel.

"Their queen? *Clara? A queen?*" Gemma choked out the words.

"Look at these!" Alistur proudly showed them the sketches Olivia had drawn.

"Clara's a queen?" Gemma whispered under her breath and stared at the sketches for a long moment, before glaring at Thurlow. "And you say you *talked* with her?"

"That is correct, Gemma," Thurlow answered. "I asked her specifically if she wished to return to Mont Renault. Miss Clara spoke freely with King Stern at her side, and she informed me with certainty that it is indeed her unwavering desire to remain with the merfolk—as Queen of the Alecians. As a matter of fact, the tribe occupies the ruins of Queen Ruthelda's summer palace. It appears she is highly respected by the tribe and I believe her position has great purpose for all of us."

"All of us?" Giles looked confused.

"Yes. I believe she will be very instrumental in orchestrating trade. And other important matters."

"Trade?" Giles asked.

"On behalf of the king, I've committed to provide the tribe with the provisions they need to remain comfortable and safe. In return, we'll receive bounties of delicacies we cannot harvest ourselves. Among other things." He didn't mention the return of the long-lost Fleurbanian treasures. "The king will see to it that the tribe is safe from fishermen and protected from the pirates trolling the coast in search of treasure. Miss Clara is now royalty. I can assure you she will be safeguarded as such."

Both Gemma and Giles simply stared at Thurlow, either in disbelief or in awe—he wasn't sure which. Looking as though they were trying to come to terms with what he was telling them, Thurlow decided there was really not much more he could say.

"We do have something for you, from Miss Clara." Thurlow nudged Alistur to open the satchel again. Gemma's eyes bulged at the exquisitely odd gift Alistur thrust toward her. "There's a letter for you to read, also." Alistur eagerly pointed to the tiny scroll tucked in the mouth of the oyster.

"Oh, and I believe she would want *you* to have this, Mr. Renwicke." Alistur handed him the scabbard holding the ruby-encrusted dagger.

"Miss Clara is indeed living a life of her choosing and I hope it brings you solace knowing she is quite happy and safe. My apologies for this most unexpected and astonishing news, but we'll leave you now with your privacy," Thurlow stated.

Thurlow and Alistur bowed their farewell and left Gemma and Giles standing on the stoop holding the sketches, the ruby-encrusted dagger, and a small fortune of jewels in their hands.

Thurlow looked back over his shoulder one more time with a parting comment. "Oh, and even though it was purely accidental—Miss Clara is nonetheless a true and radiant queen!"

ᘛ

"It's been a *very* long day, Son. Let's go home." Thurlow patted his son's back and they embarked on the short walk through the compound toward their quarters.

"It's been a long *week,* Father," Alistur sighed.

"Indeed, it has. Yesterday was intended to be only a day of triumph and jubilation. I'm very sorry you had to witness loss of life in the caverns, Son. While we can't place ourselves in his shoes, or in his frame of mind, but if given the chance, it's more than likely that man would have chosen his actions differently." Thurlow paused. "And, I'm sorry you had to experience the horrendous accident with Gustus today. He has a good soul, and I'll bet, given the chance, he *would* do it all over again." Thurlow looked his son in the eye before continuing. "Each of them suffered dire consequences while in the service to others. The choices we make throughout our lifetimes will bring about consequences. Life lessons. What we choose to salvage from those lessons is up to us," Thurlow reasoned, while his son listened intently.

"I wish I hadn't chosen the wrong wand in the blue quarry." Alistur looked at the ground as he walked. "I wonder if I would have made the same mistake if Great-grandfather had been with me? Maybe he would have led me to the right path to begin with."

"It was a mistake for sure, Son. But it did not define nor impede your ability, did it?" Thurlow asked.

"No, Father. It didn't," Alistur answered quietly.

"Perhaps it even prepared you for a greater achievement. Once you knew—*truly knew*, in your heart and soul, that you'd found the crystal that was meant for you, that's when you realized victory. Son, I've no doubt Great-grandfather was indeed with you in the caverns. He's always with us, in spirit. A great man once said: Do not follow where the path may lead. Go instead where there is no path and leave a trail."

Alistur's eyes gleamed and his heart was bursting with joy, knowing he'd made his father very proud. "Great-grandfather used to tell me that having courage is hoping for the opportunity to face your biggest fear."

"Son, Great-grandfather was right. You were indeed victorious over your biggest fear, because you had the courage to face it. I've never seen you more confident than while accomplishing that feat. And I've never been more proud of you. Tell me, what's the best thing you're looking forward to now?" Thurlow asked.

After a long sigh, Alistur answered. "Making sure I become the kind of wizard Great-grandfather would wish for me to be."

Thurlow nodded his head, massaging the silver stubble on his chin. "And what's the biggest challenge you believe you might face in that aspiration?"

With a slight chuckle, Alistur answered. "Wielding my powers with wisdom!"

"Son, without a doubt, you are gifted with powers greater than your learned skills. You will live your entire life always striving to control those powers. And look at what you've learned in just one week's time! I understand your reluctance to admit your wrongdoings, and I admire you for being brave enough to do your best to remedy them. Especially with Miss Clara. But, like I've said before, each and every day is a test. This was a week like none other. It takes extraordinary events to experience an extraordinary life. Our craft is one of yearning, and of learning. You will always be learning, always honing your skills, and you'll continue evolving into the magnificent wizard you were meant to be. And you've already proven you wield more power than me!" Thurlow's eyes twinkled. "I have a surprise for you, Son."

"A surprise?" Alistur's eyes widened with anticipation.

"It's time you learn about the Grimaldi Recordings," Thurlow announced.

"The *Recordings?"* Alistur's face flushed, realizing his father's intentions.

Thurlow nodded. "Yes, Son, the Grimaldi Recordings. It's weighed heavily on my mind, that I'm the only one holding the knowledge of how to decipher the ancient teachings. I've procrastinated, and risked too many *tomorrows*."

"How so?" Alistur questioned.

"Tomorrow is a gift, Son. Not a given."

"I understand," Alistur asserted.

"Balthazar would not be very proud of *me* if I failed in my responsibility to pass the knowledge on to you." Thurlow then put his arm around his son's shoulders, pulling him close. "So, you see, our responsibilities to learn and to teach, continue on and on, all throughout our lives."

With bittersweet reflection and thoughts of Balthazar, Alistur mused on his fondest memories of their conversations. "There's something else Great-grandfather used to say to me a lot and I'm beginning to understand what he meant."

"Oh? And what's that, Son?" Thurlow asked.

"When our earthly journey is over, let's leave this world with our jobs well done."

"Do not follow where the path may lead. Go instead where there is no path and leave a trail."

—Ralph Waldo Emerson

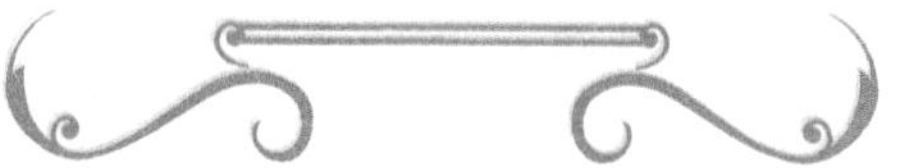

ACKNOWLEDGMENTS

I am blessed to have had the opportunity to work with Anne, Phyllis, and Brenda on this project. The collective expertise and creative talent among this team of professionals is extraordinary! With this group, nothing is truer than the adage "Teamwork makes the dream work!"

With admiration and deep respect, I give special recognition and abundant praise to the fabulous Anne Bruce, aka FAB. With numerous superpowers at her disposal, Anne has been nothing less than a Northern Star—lighting the way with unwavering encouragement and unconditional support throughout this entire journey. (And she knows just how long the journey has been.) Anne burns more midnight oil than any other mere mortal I know! If she ever tells you "I'm here for you any time, day or night," you can take it to heart, because she sincerely means it. My deepest, heartfelt gratitude goes to this remarkable woman for taking a leap of faith on this project. It's a privilege to recognize Anne as the Acquisitions Editor.

Phyllis Jask is a Rock Star in editor's clothing! She graciously accepted the ream of words I presented, and forged her way through it time and again—each time wielding a sharper tool of her trade. Low and behold, when the dust cleared, with her shape-shifting abilities, I realized Phyllis had helped to morph the pile of words I'd presented into a refined manuscript. Armed with a savvy skillset and her unique style of working from the heart, Phyllis is gifted with the ability to extract and polish the golden nuggets deeply embedded within the bones of a story. It's a privilege to recognize Phyllis as the Editorial Director on this project.

I'm pretty sure Brenda Hawkes has a crystal wand of her very own. She wields powers beyond my wildest imagination—and believe me, I do have a wild imagination! By the end of our very first conference call, Brenda could envision the big picture and was finishing my thoughts. She is truly a secret weapon! It's a privilege to recognize Brenda as the Graphic Designer on this project.

Phil Studdard, I truly believe you are related to Alistur, because you are nothing less than a wizard! Thank you for creating this magnificent cover!

Brian McElligott, thank you for sharing your superb artistic talents on this project, and for giving authenticity to the characters and beasts of Fleurbania!

Dmitriy Shvets, although it's been years since you created the map of Fleurbania, it's been a staple among the visual objects of inspiration I've kept at my fingertips throughout this journey!

I am forever grateful to my parents for giving me their lifelong blessings and encouragement to pursue my passions du jour—even though I'm certain my imagination often times tested their unconditional love and support for my endeavors. I admit, many times during the aftermath of some of my more imaginative escapades, my father would follow up with the well-worn question: *"What were you thinking?"*

Dad, as you know, my favorite bedtime stories were the ones you made up through figments of your imagination. Little did I know, those home-spun tales were previews of what was to come! Throughout my life I've seen the beauty and enjoyed the benefits of watching the two of you live your life joyfully—with generous, open hearts and helping hands. I am blessed to have these two lovebirds in my life—still holding hands and still marveling over their flock. You are my champions, and you remain my biggest supporters.

With more than a few adventures of his own under his belt and emboldened by his imagination, I see many of Alistur's characteristics in my brother. Rick, I often marvel at your self-taught skills, and I thank you for building me the best writing lair ever! It's truly my sanctuary and a place of inspiration from which to beckon my muse!

I thank my sister for her lifelong encouragement and unconditional support. Dana, you've been my biggest cheerleader throughout my life, applauding my aspirations and dreams, big or small. Ever since I can remember, you've been my best friend and accomplice, always willing to play along, and go along—whether traipsing around the country, or to far corners of the world in search of Fleurbania! Those adventures ignited my dreams with real-life possibilities—and burdened you with a lot of reading! For years I've witnessed your multitude of talents (too many to mention), but when you perfected an authentic Fleurbanian biscotti, it was then I realized you are the epitome of a modern-day Renaissance woman! Having you by my side, I know for certain my pursuits will always be well-fueled with positive encouragement—and a lot of fun!

My nieces, great-nieces, and great-nephews: Within this group is a magnificent variety of unique talents, and shenanigans! All of you have given me so much joy throughout my life, and I am so proud of each and every one of you! Thank you for indulging me in escapades around the world in pursuit of character-building quests. You are my tribe! There are many more memories yet to be made and I can hardly wait for our next adventure!

ABOUT THE AUTHOR

D.L. Winter was raised in Kansas and spent her adult life in Northern California.

Many years ago, on her first trip abroad, inspired by the nostalgic allure of legends, lore, and architectural wonders of the Mediterranean region, the concept for Alistur's story was born. However, crafting the fable would have to wait. Plotting adventures in the fictitious Kingdom of Fleurbania would be among the creative projects of her retirement. After a corporate career, D.L. now resides in her home state of Kansas once again, telling tales and enjoying life with family members.

www.ingramcontent.com/pod-product-compliance
Lightning Source LLC
Chambersburg PA
CBHW020500310726
48979CB00016B/2744/J